CONSULTING
DETECTIVE

CONSULTING
DETECTIVE

○ ○ ○

ALAN MANIFOLD

○ ○ ○

BAHÁ'Í
PUBLISHING

WILMETTE, ILLINOIS

Bahá'í Publishing
401 Greenleaf Ave, Wilmette, Illinois 60091

Copyright © 2018 by the National Spiritual Assembly
of the Bahá'ís of the United States
All rights reserved. Published 2018
Printed in the United States of America ∞
ISBN: 978-1-61851-122-5

21   20   19   18   4   3   2   1

Library of Congress Cataloging-in-Publication Data
Names: Manifold, Alan, author.
Title: Consulting detective / Alan Manifold.
Description: Wilmette, Illinois : Baha'i Publishing, 2018.
Identifiers: LCCN 2017044841 | ISBN 9781618511225 (paperback)
Subjects: LCSH: Detectives—Illinois—Fiction. | Bahai men—Fiction. |
   Rabbis—Violence against—Fiction. | Murder—Investigation—Fiction. |
   Hate crime investigation—Fiction. | Illinois—Fiction. | BISAC: FICTION /
   Mystery & Detective / General. | FICTION / Religious. | GSAFD: Mystery
   fiction.
Classification: LCC PR9619.M267 C66 2018 | DDC 823/.92—dc23
LC record available at https://lccn.loc.gov/2017044841

Cover design by Jamie Hanrahan
Book design by Patrick Falso

For Lorraine, my endless source of encouragement and love

Contents

Wednesday, Day 1

"You were fighting?" Detective Sergeant Mihdí Montgomery asked his seven-year-old son, Enoch. "Did you start it, or did the other child?"

"Dad, it wasn't like that," Enoch began to explain.

At just that moment, however, Mrs. Javad, the office secretary said, "The principal will see you now, Mr. Montgomery."

Mihdí arose from his chair and entered the principal's office, with Enoch following. "Hello, Janice. It's good to see you, although not necessarily for this reason."

"Good to see you, too, Mihdí. How's Andrea?"

"She's just fine. You know her, always busy with a million things."

"Yes, I run into her at meetings now and then, but it seems we're both always too busy to talk."

There was a brief silence, as the pleasantries had run their course.

Dr. Janice Chernievski was forty-six, the same age as Mihdí. She and Mihdí's wife, Andrea, had known each other since Janice had moved to Pine Bluff four years ago to take the job as principal of Abbott Elementary school. That acquaintanceship had grown to friendship when Enoch began attending the school. They were both heavily involved in causes of social justice in the community, particularly the empowerment of women. Janice Chernievski had only the slightest trace of an accent, inherited from her first-generation immigrant Polish parents. Dressed in a black pantsuit and white blouse, accented by a silk scarf in the browns and yellows of fall, with a welcoming smile, a high forehead, and half-moon glasses hanging on a chain around her neck, she looked every inch an education professional.

"Mihdí, I was surprised to hear that Enoch had been caught fighting, but as I learned more about it, I was less surprised. He will have to serve detention after school—that's mandatory, and I probably wouldn't release him from that if I could—but we won't take any further disciplinary action against him. I don't know if I can say the same for his opponent."

"I don't know any details about this, Janice," said Mihdí. "I got a message from the dispatcher and came right in."

"Oh, I'm sorry," the principal said. "Of course you wouldn't have heard anything yet. Enoch didn't really start the fight, and didn't even want to fight, as far as I can tell. He just wouldn't allow a bully to succeed in picking on someone."

"Well, that sounds a little better," said Mihdí.

The principal turned to Enoch and gave him a warm smile. "Do you want to tell us what happened?"

"I was playing over at the edge of the playground, and I saw Carl Sapp picking on Ruth."

"Ruth Levy," Dr. Chernievski added.

"Yeah," said Enoch. "Carl was calling her names and pushing her. She was crying."

"What did you do?" his father asked.

"I ran over there and told Carl to stop. He pushed Ruth harder and made her fall down. Then I stepped between the two of them. That's when he swung at me."

"Did he hit you?" asked the principal.

"Not very hard," the boy said. "I kinda ducked and held my arm out like this." He stood up to demonstrate. "He just hit my arm a little bit."

"Did you hit him back?"

"No, I just told him to quit, but he swung at me again. That time he hit me in the stomach. I was gonna run, but Ruth was still lying there, so I hit him back. I musta hit him in the nose, cause it started bleeding. That's when Mrs. Ayman came and brought us both in here."

The principal turned to Mihdí. "Mrs. Ayman said she saw only Enoch's punch, but she also talked to Ruth, who told her pretty much the same story that Enoch just told us."

"Enoch," Dr. Chernievski said, "you know we have rules against fighting—for any reason. You'll have to do your detention."

Enoch nodded with a somber face.

"But I think it was noble what you were trying to do. I'm sure Ruth is grateful. We'll just have to talk about other ways you might have handled the situation so that you didn't have to resort to fighting."

Enoch nodded again.

Mihdí added, "You can serve your detention proudly, Enoch. Your Mom and I can help you come up with new strategies for conflict resolution, but your first concern was for justice, and that's worth a little detention. Bahá'u'lláh says, '*The Best Beloved . . .*'"

Enoch finished the phrase, "'. . . *of all things in My sight is Justice.*'"

Mihdí smiled and gave Enoch a hug.

"You can go back to class now," the principal told the boy. "Ask Mrs. Javad for a pass."

Mihdí prepared to go as well.

"Could you stay a minute, Mihdí?" Dr. Chernievski asked.

He sat back down.

"I think you might be interested in a few more details about this," the principal said, "particularly with the trouble over at the synagogue last night."

"You certainly know how to get my attention, Janice," he replied.

"Ruth Levy is Jewish, and the names Carl called her were racial slurs—'kike,' 'yid,' and 'Jew-girl.' I can hardly imagine where he even learned those terms. That's usually something kids learn from their parents, but I've never had anything but good feelings for Mr. Sapp. He's a single father, and he's been very involved with Carl's education here. I wouldn't have guessed that he harbored any of those kinds of feelings."

"Well, perhaps I'll learn more about it tonight. I'm going to take Enoch over to apologize to Carl and try to get them both over this."

"Wow," Janice exclaimed. "I'm impressed. Most parents wouldn't do that. But I suppose with Andrea in the family, this is second nature to you folks."

"I guess that's it. Andrea has shown me that it's total realism. If kids don't learn to take responsibility for their actions and clear things up while conflicts are still small, the conflicts just grow and grow, and pretty soon we have gangs and wars."

3

"Well, I don't think this is going to lead to war, but it sounds like a good philosophy, anyway. Good luck!"

"Thanks."

They shook hands, and Mihdí returned to work.

* * *

That there had been some "trouble" at Beth Shalom Synagogue, as Dr. Chernievski had mentioned, was a serious understatement: it was a murder and a hate crime rolled into one. Rabbi Jacob Klemme had been killed by a blow to the head, apparently when he surprised someone spraying anti-Semitic slogans on the walls inside the synagogue.

Detective Mihdí Montgomery was in charge of the investigation. Montgomery's skin was light brown in color, and most people considered him African American. His father was black, but his mother was Persian. He was almost six foot four in height and reasonably trim, although the signs of a bit of belly were starting to become unmistakable over the last few years. He sported a short, neatly trimmed moustache, but no beard. His thick, curly hair was cut to an even, short length. Today, as on most work days, he was wearing a dark suit with a white, long-sleeved shirt and a conservative tie. His goal was to look presentable in virtually any venue, without standing out.

Mihdí had risen through the ranks in his fourteen years with the Pine Bluff Police Department. He had been a detective now for three years. This particular investigation had only just begun, so Mihdí had not yet turned up any witnesses, nor did he have any suspects.

He had been called over to the synagogue about 7:00 p.m. the previous evening when the rabbi's body had been discovered by a member of Beth Shalom's congregation. When he entered the sanctuary, the most striking thing was the graffiti. Slogans were spray-painted across three walls in large letters. "Death to Jews," said the one on the right side of the pews. "Christ-killers," read the one along the back wall. "Free Palestine," read the third, blazoned across the left sanctuary wall. In addition to the writing, there were large swastikas crudely painted on the two side walls. The rabbi's body was lying next to one of the walls where a slogan was painted. An ornate brass candleholder was lying near the body, with traces of what looked like hair and blood on it. A police photographer was taking pictures of the entire crime scene. Shortly after Mihdí arrived, Officer Beth Carr arrived to process the crime scene more thoroughly. The city was too small to have a separate forensics squad or evidence lab, but Beth had been trained in evidence gathering and handled most of the serious crime scenes.

Someone from the coroner's office came and did a quick evaluation before confirming that the cause of death appeared to be homicide. He had the rabbi's body sent to a local hospital for an autopsy to be performed the next day.

Mihdí had interviewed Scott Craig, the man who had discovered the rabbi's body. Craig, who was a member of the congregation, said that he had come for a meeting with Rabbi Klemme at Klemme's invitation. When he arrived at the synagogue at 6:00 p.m., he saw the graffiti painted on the sanctuary wall as he walked past it toward the doorway leading to the synagogue's administrative area. It was dark enough that he had not seen the rabbi's body right away. He had then run to the office to check on the rabbi. He found no disruption of the office area, but neither did he find Rabbi Klemme. He returned to the sanctuary, thinking that Klemme might be already working to get the graffiti removed. It was then that he discovered the rabbi's body near the wall, past the door into the office area, further toward the front of the sanctuary. He called the police from his cell phone and waited outside until they arrived a short time later.

The detective had done a quick check of the office area himself and found that the rabbi's computer was still on and was opened to his e-mail and calendar program. Montgomery checked and found that there was, indeed, a meeting scheduled for 6:00 p.m. with Scott Craig. Thinking there was little more to be learned, he let Craig go home about 9:00 p.m. and went home himself as well.

*   *   *

First thing Wednesday morning, several hours before his meeting with Janice Chernievski at Enoch's school, Mihdí had arranged for police officers to canvass the neighborhood to try to track down any witnesses to the crime.

He also received and reviewed preliminary news about the autopsy, consulted with Beth Carr about the evidence, and wrote up the main facts of the case to identify the primary directions for his investigation. He had other cases he was working on, but his captain had told him to set aside those that could wait and to pass on to other detectives any that couldn't so that Mihdí would be able to devote full time to this investigation. Murders were not common in Pine Bluff, so each one was treated as a very serious matter.

Pine Bluff, Illinois was not a large town, but as a suburb of Chicago, it reflected many of the trends, both good and bad, of much larger cities. The crime rate in Pine Bluff was lower than that of Chicago but higher than that of comparably sized cities in rural settings. Recently, the city had been combating a steep increase in apparent gang activity, as well as significant drug-related crime. To date, there had been no hate crimes related to an increasing population of immigrants, but the police were monitoring inter-ethnic tensions to make sure no such problems arose.

After his other cases were referred to other detectives, Mihdí reviewed photographs of the crime scene. Mihdí looked at the pictures of the graffiti and found something very odd about them. While the two anti-Semitic slogans fit together, the third one, "Free Palestine," struck him as out of place. The first two suggested racial or religious hatred, while the third was more of a political statement. He made a note to himself to ponder this strange juxtaposition later.

He found close-ups of the candleholder that was presumed to be the murder weapon. The first reports from Beth Carr and the coroner indicated that the blood found on it was the same type as the rabbi's, although more tests would be needed to prove it was definitely his. The candleholder was quite ornate, and had spaces for eight small candles and one slightly larger one in the center. "A hanukkia," Mihdí mused. "A bit early for that, I'd think."

The initial autopsy report indicated that the cause of death was head trauma caused by a blow from behind with a heavy object. This all seemed to confirm that Jacob Klemme had been struck with the hanukkia. The weight of the heavy brass hanukkia made it impossible to determine how large a person had wielded the object to strike the blow; even the smallest and weakest person could have hit very hard. Time of death was set between about 1:00 and 4:00 p.m. on Tuesday, the day the body was discovered.

Beth Carr reported that no fingerprints or other identifying evidence had been found. Some hairs, stained with red, had been recovered from the wall just above where the body was found. The hairs were the same color as Rabbi Klemme's hair, and it appeared that he had hit the wall on the way to the floor. She had sent them to a forensics lab to be processed, just in case. No spray paint cans or other evidence associated with the crime had been found at or near the synagogue.

Detective Kurt Childs, one of the newest members of the Pine Bluff police force, had been assigned to check with people from each of the businesses on the block around the synagogue. When he returned to the police station a bit after noon, he reported that nobody had noticed anything suspicious. Business had gone on as usual. Nobody seemed to have acted oddly, nobody who had a routine seemed to have varied it, and nothing out of the ordinary had happened until the police arrived at about 6:30 p.m.

Mihdí made a call to Sam Schliebaum, the President of Congregation Beth Shalom, and made arrangements to meet him at the synagogue. The building had been sealed after the rabbi's body had been removed, but there was no current police activity. Mihdí went out the back door of the police department and got into his blue Mini Cooper S, the model with a Union Jack painted on the roof. He arrived first at the synagogue and used the key the police had borrowed to let himself in. He had another opportunity to see the spray-painted graffiti before the congregation president arrived.

After just a few minutes, an elderly gentleman entered the building. Sam Schliebaum looked good for eighty-seven, but he walked slowly and deliberately. He removed his coat and held it over his arm. He did not remove his hat. He wore a brown pinstriped suit that looked a few years out of date but in good shape. The ensemble included a maroon tie with a full Windsor knot that made the tie hang a little short. Schliebaum's face was heavily wrinkled, and his hair was white.

"Ah, Mr. Schliebaum." Mihdí offered his hand to the man.

"I'm afraid your name has slipped my mind, young man," said Samuel Schliebaum. "The memory is none too good these days, I'm sorry to say."

"Mihdí Montgomery," the detective said.

"Oh, of course. You're with the local Bahá'í community, aren't you?"

7

"That's right. We met at an interfaith service five or six years ago down at the park."

"I remember. That was a lovely service. Weren't you the organizer?"

"I was one of them," Mihdí replied, modestly. "There was a whole committee, of course. It's more than one person could do. I'd say your memory is working just fine, Mr. Schliebaum."

The older man grinned. "Well, I haven't lost it all yet, I guess."

"I appreciate your agreeing to meet me here," Mihdí said.

"I have been wanting to have a chance to talk to whomever was running the investigation," Schliebaum replied. "I'm glad to find that it's you. Would you like to go to the office and sit and talk?"

"That would be great, Mr. Schliebaum. Please lead the way."

Mihdí reviewed some of the facts of the case with the congregation president, then asked him to talk about the rabbi. "He was fairly new here, wasn't he?" Mihdí asked.

"Been here just six months or so, I think," Schliebaum replied. "Before that he was at a synagogue in Ohio—I'm afraid I can't dredge up the name of the place right now. He was a very likable young man, and hard-working, too. He took his job very seriously."

"Did he seem to be getting along well here? Fitting in and connecting with the congregation?"

"Why do you ask? It's a pretty cut and dried case from the sound of it. Is there more to this that you haven't told me?"

"Nothing particular, no. It's just that I can't just stop at the front door of a case," Mihdí replied. "I have to go in and look around to make sure I'm not missing anything."

"Oh, that's all right then. Yes, he was getting along very well. He treated us old-timers with respect and honored the traditions of the temple, but he also seemed to relate to the younger people. More of them have been showing up lately, and I think it's because of him."

"This is sort of a side issue," Montgomery said, "but can you clarify for me the relationship between the terms congregation, synagogue, and temple? I thought I remembered that the term *temple* was reserved for the ancient one in Jerusalem."

"That's true for the orthodox congregations. They'll call themselves a congregation and generally call their place of worship a *shul*, and they don't use the term *temple* at all. The reformed Jews usually call their places *temples*. This is a conservative synagogue, sort of a compromise for when there's only enough of us for a single congregation. Officially, we stick with the term *synagogue*, but I'm a reformed Jew myself, and they all mean pretty much the same thing to me."

"Sorry for the tangent. I like learning."

"No problem, Detective Montgomery. I like talking, so we're a good match." Both men laughed.

"Obviously nothing like this has ever happened before here, but there have been some unpleasant incidents in the past, haven't there?"

"Unfortunately, yes. Over the last two years we've had, I think, three different attacks by vandals. In each case, they spray-painted their garbage on the front of the building or the doors."

"I hate to make you repeat the words, but I think it would help me to know what was written."

Mr. Schliebaum sighed. "I've heard this garbage all my life, son. I don't have any problem repeating it. Once they wrote 'Hitler was right,' and once it was, 'Death to Jewish pigs.' The third time, there were no words, only swastikas. One of them was even carved into the door that time. Luckily, it wasn't very deep, and it could be repaired fairly easily. Had to stain the doors a lot darker, though, to hide it."

"I'm so sorry, Mr. Schliebaum," Mihdí said. "It makes me sad that anyone in this community would be so sick that they would do that kind of thing."

"Jews are used to persecution, son. We've grown tough. But it's hard to see a nice young man like Rabbi Klemme lost. It'll be a blow to the congregation, make no mistake."

"Could you tell me a little about Jacob Klemme, Mr. Schliebaum?" Mihdí asked. "What kind of person he was, how he spent his time, whether he was married? Anything you can think of would be of interest."

"I'll tell you what I know," Schliebaum replied. "You might do best to talk to some of the younger members of the congregation as well, since I believe he spent a great deal of time with them."

"Yes, of course," Mihdí replied.

"I believe he grew up in New York City," Schliebaum began. "At least I know his parents are living there now. His degree is from JTS, which is also in the city."

"That's the Jewish Theological Seminary?" Mihdí asked.

"Very good, young man," answered Schliebaum. "Didn't know if you would know what that is."

"A little test, then, eh?" chuckled Mihdí.

"I guess so, now that you say that," confirmed Schliebaum. "His first synagogue was near Pittsburgh, I believe. He was there only a couple of years then moved to the synagogue in Lorain, Ohio. That's where he was when we hired him."

"That's on the lake, east of Cleveland, I think, right?"

"That sounds about right. It's been a long time since I traveled out that way, but I think that's right. It took us a while to find him, once we started our search. He's been here about half a year now. I remember he started on April 15th—tax day."

"Where did he live?" Mihdí asked.

"He has an apartment here in Pine Bluff," answered Schliebaum. "I haven't been there, but he said it's just a short walk from here. Some of the folks that helped move him in said the whole place is just wall-to-wall books. That's a typical rabbi for you, I guess."

"Perhaps I'm a rabbi and don't know it," Mihdí joked.

Schliebaum laughed. "I think there's a bit of rabbi in all of us. Or there should be, anyway."

"Did Rabbi Klemme have any special friends in the congregation?" Mihdí inquired. "Either people who knew him from before or people with whom he had a special bond?"

"He seemed to make friends easily," Schliebaum replied. "But of course there's Tammy."

"Tammy was a special friend?" Mihdí asked. "Is she a member of the congregation? What is her full name?"

"Tammy Ornstein," Schliebaum replied. "Tamar Ornstein, actually. She's the daughter of a couple that have been members here for a number of years.

She lives up in Downers Grove, but she still comes here for services. She and Jacob hit it off immediately and have been going together pretty heavily almost the whole time he's been here. I think she broke off an engagement with someone else even."

"That sounds pretty serious," Mihdí said. "I'd better talk to her right away."

"Here's a copy of the synagogue directory you can have," Schliebaum offered as he reached up to a box on a nearby shelf and pulled out a small booklet. "Tammy should be listed in there."

"Thank you for that," Mihdí said.

"Tammy is probably twenty-five or so," Schliebaum said. "She was one of a whole group of kids around that age that have grown up together. Several of them still come here. Since Jacob has been here, a few more have started attending regularly again. One or two of them are married, but it seems like they're mostly single. I'd say that group was Jacob's main crowd, particularly with his connection to Tammy. In addition to that crowd, Jacob had started an "Introduction to Judaism" class that had a couple of people attending. And there was the daily minyan, which attracts mostly older folks like me. We had a period of eight or nine months when we didn't have a rabbi here, after Rabbi Horwitz retired. I hadn't realized how much more vibrant a synagogue is with an energetic rabbi. I guess we have to start that journey all over again now."

"Yes, I understand that can be a long, hard process," Mihdí said.

"How do you Bahá'ís get new ministers or whatever you have?" Schliebaum asked. "Do you have to do a big search like we do, or does someone just appoint them, like the Methodists do?"

"There's no clergy in the Bahá'í Faith," Mihdí said. "So we avoid the whole ordeal of having to find clergy. But the trade-off is that we all have to share the responsibility for making sure the community stays vibrant."

"Interesting," Schliebaum replied. "I don't envy you that. In any case, it will take a while for this congregation to recover."

"I wish you the best of luck," Mihdí said. "I believe we're done here, Mr. Schliebaum. And I think we've gotten all the information we can from the crime scene, so I'll ask to have all traces of our presence removed as soon as possible. Hopefully, you can get back to some degree of normalcy here. I'll be in touch, though."

* * *

Mihdí called Tammy Ornstein and arranged to meet her at her home in Downers Grove that afternoon.

Detective Kurt Childs had already canvassed the neighborhood and asked if anyone had seen anything or knew anything about the murder, but Mihdí wanted to gather a bit of intelligence on his own, and in his own way. There was a coffee shop right next to the synagogue, so he went in and ordered a decaf cappuccino. There were only a few customers at that time of day.

Mihdí struck up a conversation with the man who had served him, who turned out to be the owner, Ahmad Muhammad. Muhammad was thin but not too tall, and his skin tone was nearly the same light brown as Mihdí's. He wore a gray t-shirt and jeans, but with a white apron over the ensemble. Mihdí complimented him on the coffee and on the atmosphere of the coffee shop.

"It was a dream of my father's to come to America and open such a shop," the shop owner told him. "But he died at home in Tunisia before he was able to make it a reality. I did it partly for him."

"I believe family is very important in Arab culture," Mihdí offered.

"Friendships, alliances—all of these things can pass, but family is a constant." As Muhammad spoke about family, he drew himself up to his full height.

Mihdí nodded. "I'm with the police force, a detective. I'm sure someone already asked you whether you saw or heard anything about the murder next door."

Ahmad nodded. "I wasn't here that day; my nephew, Azdeen, was watching the shop. Azdeen couldn't think of anything unusual from that evening, and I couldn't think of anything from the day before."

"Actually," Mihdí interrupted, "it appears that the murder took place sometime Tuesday afternoon. The body was discovered not too long after that."

Ahmad took that in. "I can ask Azdeen if he saw anything then," he said, "but I think the police asked him about everything from that entire day. I've been keeping my eyes and ears open since then, but I haven't heard anything out of the ordinary. It's such a shame. The rabbi was a nice man. He came over here often to get coffee. I make sure to stock several foods that are certified kosher since we're right next to a synagogue, but the rabbi usually just had coffee. He'd often sit and chat a while, either with me or with some of the regulars. Everybody liked him. I'll miss him, personally. If I hear anything, I'll be sure to let you know. "

"I imagine you told the police where you were on Tuesday afternoon?" Mihdí asked. "I hate to ask, but it's my job."

"Of course," replied Ahmad. "I was on a buying trip downtown. I gave the contact numbers to the other detectives if you want to follow up."

"It's routine to follow up," Mihdí informed him. "Detective Childs has probably already done so."

"Well, I hope something comes up to help you catch whoever it was. Murdering a nice man like that is a crime against all of us."

"I'll do my best," Mihdí said. "Keep me in your prayers."

"You can count on that, Detective."

Mihdí walked past the other businesses on the block, which included a music store and a Christian bookstore, interspersed with a few empty properties, and finally ended up in a Jewish deli at the very end of the block. He ordered dessert and a drink and had just finished paying when he recognized one of the people behind the counter.

"Harry Katz, you old dog! I didn't know you worked here."

Harry Katz had reached retirement age a while ago, but he wore his years well. His hair showed some gray here and there but was still predominantly black. His complexion was light—almost unhealthy looking—and he had no facial hair. He was rather slight, both short and thin, but seemed to have wiry muscles under his wrinkled skin. He had a small, sparsely decorated black kippah pinned to his hair in the back, and he was wearing a brown plaid flannel shirt, khaki pants, and worn brown loafers.

Harry ambled out from behind the counter. "I only started working here in January," he said after they had shaken hands and found a table. "It's part time, and Neil gives me first pick of hours, so it's pretty ideal. I'm officially retired, but a man can't sit at home all day. I'm not sure who would go crazy first, me or Marilyn."

"I'm sure Marilyn was overjoyed to have you at home," Mihdí replied.

"Oh, she was," Katz said. "I started to think she had been saving up projects for me since the day we were married. I was working harder at home than I had worked at my job. I was almost ready to start going to the gym or something to get some rest. Luckily, I found this job instead."

They both laughed.

"I'm working on the Klemme case, Harry."

"I had heard that. There aren't too many secrets in a neighborhood like this, although it's not what it used to be."

"How so?" Mihdí asked.

"This used to be the heart and center of the Jewish community. There was the synagogue, of course; it's been located here for many years. But most of the shops on this block and many of the surrounding blocks were owned and run by Jews. Much of the community lived within walking distance, and they really did all of their business right here."

"When did that change?" Mihdí prompted.

"It was a gradual thing, I guess. New businesses have encroached a bit on the old residential sections, so some of the community moved out a bit farther. They mostly still came to the synagogue, but they just lived a bit farther away. With fewer Jews in the neighborhood, some of the Jewish businesses weren't doing quite as well. They moved to strip malls and to other suburbs, where they could afford bigger and nicer places, and tried to appeal to a wider clientele. Suddenly, this community was no longer a Jewish community anymore. There are at least as many Arabs as Jews now, as well as Blacks, and Latinos, and Asians—you name it, we got it. Actually, I say *we*, but I don't live in this area, either. Marilyn and I moved over to Lockport, west of you folks."

"I remember when you moved up there. Must have been what, three or four years ago?"

Katz nodded.

Mihdí continued, "Has there been any trouble between the groups?"

14

"Surprisingly, no," Harry told him. "If the world could get along as well as this neighborhood, we'd be in good shape."

"That's good to hear."

Mihdí's cell phone rang, and he excused himself to answer it.

"I'm sorry, Harry," Mihdí said when the phone call was concluded. "The police dispatcher says that Enoch's school called and that they need me to come over there for something or other."

"Give your kids a kiss for me, Mihdí. How old are they now?"

"Enoch is seven, and Lua is five."

"Oh, my! Time does fly by, doesn't it? My Josh turned forty this year, and his kids are both in high school. I thought things would slow down when I got older, but it seems the world is spinning faster and faster. Don't miss any opportunities to spend time with your kids, Mihdí. All too soon you'll be wondering where the time went."

* * *

When Mihdí had finished his conversation with Janice Chernievski at Enoch's school, he had just enough time to make it to Downers Grove for his appointment with Tammy Ornstein. She came to the door quickly after he rang the bell.

Tamar Ornstein was dressed in jeans and a sweatshirt. She was perhaps a bit shorter than average but not slight. Her hair was a dark brown and very curly and thick. Sam Schliebaum had said she was about twenty-five, but Mihdí would have guessed she was a bit older. Her smile was sincere but a bit strained. It was obvious from the redness and puffiness around her eyes that she had been crying.

After they were both seated in Tammy's living room, Mihdí said, "I'm very sorry for your loss, Miss Ornstein. I understand you and Rabbi Klemme were close friends."

"Yes, we were. I can't believe Jacob's really dead."

"Do you have someone you can talk to about it at this difficult time?"

"Thanks, yeah. My parents still live in Pine Bluff, and I have lots of friends I can talk to as well."

15

"May I ask you some questions?"

"Of course," she answered. "I don't know how I can help you, but I'll be happy to try."

"Can you describe Jacob for me a bit?" Mihdí asked. "I need to get a picture of who he was in order to try to find out if there is more to this crime than the obvious."

"I'm sorry," Tammy said. "I don't really know the details of what happened."

"Oh, I apologize, of course you wouldn't know anything about it. It appears that Rabbi Klemme surprised a vandal in the synagogue sanctuary and was struck in the head. We don't yet have many more details than that."

"That's horrible," Tammy said, and began to cry.

"It's utterly incomprehensible," agreed Mihdí. "I'll never be able to understand how one person could do such a thing to another. Do they not realize that we're all God's perfect creations?"

Tammy looked at him with some surprise. "Funny to hear that sort of sentiment from a policeman. I'd have thought you'd be, oh, I don't know, hardened to this sort of thing."

"I think too many of us are. I hope I never get so inured to the inhumanity of murder that it doesn't kick me in the gut at least a little."

They sat in silence for a moment before Mihdí said, "Could you tell me a bit about Jacob?"

Tammy thought for a moment, as if organizing her thoughts. "He was really present. I think that's the first word I would use to describe him. Wherever he was, whoever he was with, he was always completely there, as if there was nothing else for him to think about in the entire world. It really made me feel special when he spent time with me. But it wasn't just with me; he was like that for everyone."

Mihdí nodded but didn't say anything.

"I don't know what you know about Judaism and rabbis, but they're not quite the same as Christian ministers. Their primary duty is to study, to be scholars. Because they have studied so much, people come to them for advice and guidance and stuff. But they don't have any responsibility for other people's spiritual development or anything. It's just that they get to be Jewish full-time, so to say, so they're maybe better at it than the rest of us. But Jacob was really humble about what he knew. He didn't approach things as if he was the only one who would know the answers and everyone else should just listen. It was more like a collaboration between equals. So I think the older members at Beth Shalom liked the fact that he honored their experience and wisdom. And the younger ones never felt talked down to, so they were very comfortable with him as well."

"How did he spend his days?" Mihdí asked.

"I guess most days he worked in his office a lot of the day," she answered. "In addition to studying and being a sort of spiritual guide, he was the only full-time employee of the congregation, so he took care of routine office matters, kept files, took care of business—that sort of thing. He also did a lot of reading at the office. Oh, and he prepared his sermons there. I don't know how long all of that stuff took him each week. Whenever others were around, he dropped everything and was with us—fully present, like I said."

"May I ask about your relationship with him?" Mihdí asked softly.

"Well, we'd only known each other since he arrived in the spring, but we had become a couple. We had even been talking about marriage."

Mihdí paused a moment, then said, "I believe I heard that you had been engaged to someone else and had broken that off recently . . ."

Tammy looked uncomfortable. "That's basically true. A few months after Jacob moved here, I started to realize that the guy I was engaged to was not such a good match. I had felt a spark with Jacob, and I wanted to be free to pursue a relationship with him if he was interested. Jacob told me later that he had felt the same kind of spark but had kept a bit of distance out of respect for my commitment to Scott."

"Scott?" Mihdí questioned.

"That's right, Scott Craig. That's my ex's name."

"He's also a member of the congregation, is that right?"

"Yes, he is. He and I have known each other since we were quite young."

"When you broke up with him, how did Scott take the news?"

Tammy looked down and answered quietly, "Well, he wasn't happy about it. I think we had both assumed for years that we'd end up together. This was a bit of an upset to both our life plans."

"Did he appear to hold a grudge against Rabbi Klemme for stealing you away?"

Tammy gave Mihdí a quick glance and shook her head nervously. "Oh, no, he would never do anything like that."

"When was the last time you saw Mr. Craig?" Mihdí asked.

She looked down at her hands. "I see him at services sometimes. I wasn't there last Saturday, but it might have been the week before."

"Have you talked to him since then?"

Tammy shook her head but didn't say anything.

Mihdí gave her a little time, but she didn't elaborate.

"When was the last time you saw or spoke to Jacob?" he asked.

"He had dinner here with me on Monday," she said. "We may have spoken on the phone on Tuesday, but it was nothing significant—I don't remember a call. That could only have been in the morning if we did talk, because I was in meetings at work from noon until quitting time." She looked as if she might start crying again.

Mihdí smiled and patted her hand. "Thank you very much for your time, Miss Ornstein. I want to say again how sorry I am for your loss." He handed her his card and said, "If you think of anything else that you think I might want to know, here is my number. I can see myself out."

* * *

That evening after dinner, Mihdí and Enoch got in the car and drove over to Carl Sapp's house. Enoch hung back a bit as Mihdí rang the doorbell.

Mr. Sapp looked curious as to why an unknown black man stood on his porch, but he opened the door and asked what Mihdí wanted.

"This is Enoch Montgomery, Mr. Sapp, and I'm his dad. May we come in?"

Sapp nodded in recognition of the names and invited them both in. "Beer?" he offered to Mihdí.

"No thanks, I don't drink."

"How about a Coke or a Sprite, then?"

"Sprite would be great."

Mr. Sapp turned to Enoch. "Coke or Sprite for you, son?"

Enoch turned to his father, who nodded his approval. "Yes, please, sir, a Sprite," Enoch said.

Rick Sapp was a bit shorter than Mihdí, but he was very solid looking and probably outweighed Mihdí by ten or twenty pounds, just from the density of muscle. Mihdí thought that Sapp was probably a bit younger than himself—probably right around forty. He wore navy sweatpants and a gray t-shirt with a Chicago Bears logo on it. He looked like he had some kind of exercise regime, as he showed no sign of a gut and moved gracefully when he walked.

When Mr. Sapp returned with the sodas, Mihdí took a drink, then opened the conversation.

"Mr. Sapp . . ." he began.

Sapp interrupted, "Please call me Rick."

Mihdí replied, "And I'm Mihdí."

Rick's face showed confusion, and he turned one ear toward Mihdí. "I'm sorry, I didn't get your name."

"That's understandable," Mihdí replied. "It's certainly not a common one around here. It's Mihdí, spelled M-I-H-D-I, but you can pronounce it pretty much as if it were M-E-H-D-I. The 'h' doesn't really sound like a 'k,' but it's aspirated, a bit like the German 'ch.'"

"Mech-di," Rick attempted, with a bit more German "ch" than was called for.

"Close enough," said Mihdí and they both laughed. "Rick, I understand our boys got into a little fight today. I don't care what it was about; I think Enoch owes Carl an apology."

"And vice versa, I'd say. Let me call Carl." He called upstairs, "Carl, can you come down for a minute?"

Carl had apparently been eavesdropping at the top of the stairs because he appeared almost instantly when he was called.

Enoch got up and walked over to Carl as he came down the stairs into the living room. "I'm sorry that I hit you, Carl. I hope you're okay."

Carl said, "Yeah, I'm alright. I'm sorry I hit you, too."

They both stood there looking at each other for a minute, then Carl turned to his dad and said, "Dad, can he come up to my room?"

"Of course," his father replied.

Carl turned back to Enoch. "I've got some candy left over from Halloween up in my room. Wanna come up?"

Enoch nodded, and the two seven-year-olds flew up the stairs and disappeared around the corner.

"I'm glad that worked out so easily," Mihdí said. "I think it's always a good idea to make up as soon as possible so little incidents don't get blown out of proportion."

"That's a great idea," Rick replied. "I never even thought of it myself, but it sure looks like it worked out."

The two men sipped their sodas for a moment, then Rick said, "I couldn't get into school today on account of working, but the principal called me when I got home to tell me what the whole thing was about. I don't know what's gotten into that boy."

"Dr. Chernievski didn't think it would have come from you, from the conversations she's had with you."

"Most likely came from his brother, Andy. He seems to have gotten hooked up with some kind of bad crowd—skinheads, practically."

"Really? Here in town?"

"I honestly don't know. Andy's seventeen, and he won't talk about it with me. I just saw some literature in his room, and I've overheard bits of a few phone conversations. I didn't know he'd been sharing it with Carl."

Mihdí shook his head sympathetically. "If there's anything I can do, please feel free to contact me. I know that must be somewhat scary."

Rick didn't reply and just sat thoughtfully for a short while. "Are you a sports fan, Mr. Montgomery?"

"Please, call me Mihdí. And I have to admit I'm not much of a fan. I see you've got some Bears stuff up on the wall. What do you think of their chances this year?"

That was enough to get Sapp talking, so they discussed football for a few more minutes while they finished their sodas, then Mihdí arose. "I think I'd better get Enoch home. He'll need to unwind a bit before he'll be able to sleep tonight. But I think he has a new friend."

"I hope so," said Mr. Sapp.

Thursday, Day 2

The next morning, the weather had taken a turn for the worse. It felt at least ten degrees cooler, and there was rain in the forecast for the afternoon. Mihdí dropped Enoch off at school and Lua at her day care, then he went to his office, where he entered his notes from the previous day into the computer.

He checked in with his boss, Captain Sterling, to fill him in on his talk with Rick Sapp. Sterling was sixty and, as a thirty-nine-year veteran of the force, was in his last year before a planned retirement. He was white, with thick silver hair and dark plastic-rimmed glasses. He wore a small hearing aid in his left ear as a result of being too close to a gunshot when he was relatively new to the police. His formerly athletic physique was no longer so impressive because he had put on a few pounds around his midsection, and the extra weight was showing in his clean-shaven face as well. Even though he was nearing retirement, Captain Sterling was still very focused and involved with the work of his detectives.

Mihdí filled the captain in on what he had learned about Andy Sapp. Although Mihdí didn't know which group Andy had gotten mixed up with, it seemed a reasonable possibility that there was some connection to the case. The captain agreed and suggested that Mihdí check with the department's expert on gangs and juvenile crime when he got a chance. Sterling also agreed with Mihdí's idea that the Captain of Patrol be asked to send additional patrol cars up and down the street where Andy Sapp lived. Both the detective and the captain thought it wouldn't hurt to pay closer attention to his activities. They thought the increased police presence might even convince the boy to rethink his association with his racist friends.

After returning to his office, Mihdí dialed another friend, Raymond Engel, a member of a Jewish congregation in a nearby suburb.

"Ray, I'd like to pick your brain if I could," Mihdí said. "Do you have a few minutes?"

"No problem, Mihdí. What's up?"

"I imagine you know that I'm working on the Klemme murder case."

"Yes, I'd heard. I always say there's telegraph and telephone, but neither one is as fast as tell-a-Jew."

Mihdí chuckled. "I'm just wondering if you have any ideas about the case: anybody who might want the rabbi dead, any infighting in the congregation or anything like that."

"So, it's not as clear-cut as it appears? I thought it was just vandalism gone bad. That's certainly what the paper implied."

"That's the obvious conclusion, and I don't have much to go on to tell me that it's wrong, but I can't just jump to a conclusion without investigating, I guess."

"Well, there's always politics in a Jewish congregation, so there's always factions and conflicts and such. But I don't know of anything out of the ordinary at Beth Shalom. Pretty much the same folks have been arguing there for thirty years. I don't think they'd come to blows, let alone to murder.

"They did have one big issue there last year," continued Engel. "After Rabbi Horwitz retired to Phoenix, some members of the congregation were interested in selling the building and moving the synagogue out closer to the country club rather than in the downtown area. They're an old congregation. And I don't mean old just in the sense that the congregation has been in the city forever. The members are old, too. The average age there must be well into the sixties, maybe even into the seventies. The old members keep coming, but the younger folks either don't go to Temple, or they prefer to attend one closer to their homes. I think Sam Schliebaum's the current president—he must be almost eighty-five by now, and he's not doing all that well."

"He complained about his memory when I met with him yesterday," Mihdí offered.

"No doubt. And they still think he's the best one to be elected to lead the congregation. That says something in itself, I'd say."

"Why didn't they sell last year?"

"There was the selling faction, but there was another group, led by Schliebaum, that wanted to try to revitalize the congregation. They thought that if they got a fresh, young rabbi, he might attract some of the younger Jews back to Beth Shalom. It was a pretty close vote, I understand, but Schliebaum won. They went out looking and hired Jacob Klemme as soon as they found him."

"How was it working out?"

"From all I hear, it was working out just the way Schliebaum hoped it would," Ray told him. "Rabbi Klemme was really good with the older folks in the congregation, but he was best when he was working with younger people. He wasn't married, and the idea of marrying a rabbi still appeals to some of the young ladies. But he was great with couples, too. My temple has lost a few young families to Beth Shalom. They had roots there, but they had been attending Beth Elohim lately. I wonder if they'll keep going now that Rabbi Klemme is dead."

"That's very interesting information, Ray. Thanks for sharing it."

"My pleasure. Say, why don't we get together for lunch sometime soon?"

"That sounds nice," Mihdí replied. "I'll call you after Thanksgiving to set something up."

"Till then. Bye."

Since Mihdí was in the office, he took the opportunity to talk to Lieutenant Darla Brownlee, the department's expert on gang and juvenile activity. He found her in her office. She was dressed in a dark blue suit with a white blouse and was wearing small diamond studs in her pierced ears. She had a scarf tied over her voluminous hair. Her skin was a medium brown, almost mocha, and her nails were immaculately painted with miniature cornucopias for November. She wore a dark lipstick that complemented her skin tone. Her eyes, heavily made up with mascara, liner, and shadow, were fixed on Mihdí as he talked, apparently trying to extract as much information as possible from each word.

Mihdí greatly respected Darla Brownlee, who was comfortable with her lieutenant's rank but didn't let it stop her from being friendly with officers of all grades. He knew she spent some of her off hours working with disadvantaged kids in south Chicago.

He conveyed briefly to her the information he had heard from Rick Sapp about the people Sapp's son, Andy, was involved with. Brownlee listened carefully, asking questions as Mihdí laid everything out. Unfortunately, Mihdí did not know the answers to many of them.

"They could be skinheads," Brownlee said when he had finished, "but there's not much here to go on. There's at least one known skinhead sympathizer in town, a guy who's gotten some police attention in the past. In fact, we checked him out maybe five or six months ago after the last incident of vandalism at the synagogue. He had a solid alibi, so it didn't go anywhere."

Mihdí asked, "Is there evidence that there's an active group in town or nearby?"

"There's some evidence," the lieutenant told him, "but we don't have anything solid. There have been some other incidents of vandalism, but nothing serious. Certainly nothing like a murder."

She showed him a file she had been collecting on the local guy and on the national group with whom she believed he was associating. It was a fairly thin file. Mihdí noticed a crudely done flyer with some racist ranting, but there was nothing specifically anti-Semitic in it. He also saw a photo of the guy, whose name was Brent Wiegand. His head was shaved, and he had tattoos on his neck, face, and arms as well as some piercings.

"Hardly indistinguishable from any number of high school students around here," remarked Mihdí.

Brownlee nodded her agreement. "This is probably a red herring in your case," she said. "There's not enough evidence to even suggest their interest, let alone their involvement."

"I think I agree," said Montgomery, "but I've asked for some extra patrol cars to drive past Andy Sapp's house now and then, just to put them on notice. Perhaps they can swing by this Wiegand's place now and then, too."

"I'd say that much is justified," Brownlee agreed.

Mihdí thought it was a good idea to talk to Sam Schliebaum again, so he dialed his home number. His wife answered and said that he was at the synagogue. Mihdí hopped into his Mini and drove there. The police tape had all been removed. Mihdí tried the door and found that it was unlocked, so he went on inside. He entered the sanctuary quietly and saw the congregation president in a pew near the front, apparently absorbed in prayer or reflection.

"Wouldn't hurt me to say a prayer or two as well," thought Mihdí. He slipped into a pew at the back on the far side from the door and began silently repeating over and over a Bahá'í prayer revealed by the Báb: *"Is there any Remover of difficulties save God? Say: Praised be God! He is God! All are His servants, and all abide by His bidding!"*

Mihdí had found this practice very helpful in the past. He focused on the prayer, letting the words flow through him and fill his mind. As with any form of meditation, it sometimes washed away distractions that might be obstructing his thoughts, giving him an opportunity to start fresh. With his conscious thought occupied, his subconscious could sometimes reorder the facts of a case and reveal them in a slightly different light.

Both of the men were still praying when another man entered the sanctuary. Mihdí could not come up with the man's name, although he looked familiar. The man spotted Sam Schliebaum and called to him as he walked up to the front of the sanctuary, apparently unaware of Mihdí's presence. "You can stop praying now, Sam. Our prayers have already been answered."

"What do you mean, Abe?" the congregation president asked as he got to his feet. "Exactly which prayer has been answered?"

"Charlie Richardson still wants to buy the building," the man replied. "He said his offer from last year still stands. That should be enough to allow us to build elsewhere."

Mihdí saw Schliebaum's scowl and thought he ought to make his presence known before the two of them got into it. He got up noisily and the others turned to look at him.

"Didn't know you were here, Detective," Schliebaum said.

"You seemed to be praying when I came in, so I thought I'd just do a little of that myself. So, the congregation is planning to sell, eh?"

"We should have done it last year," the new man said. "Rabbi Klemme's death looks to me like a clear sign that it's time to move out of this area."

"Do you know Abe Cohen, the treasurer of our congregation?" Sam Schliebaum asked Mihdí.

Mihdí shook hands with Cohen, who looked to be not young, but younger than Schliebaum, probably in his seventies. He wore a lightweight argyle sweater over a golf shirt with a yellow collar. While Schliebaum was short, Cohen was tall. Schliebaum had thinning white hair, while Cohen was almost completely bald. Schliebaum was somewhat frail with the skinny limbs and face of age, but Cohen still had a distinctly athletic tone to his body, with muscular arms under his sweater.

"The congregation hasn't had a chance to discuss it yet, Abe," Schliebaum said to Cohen with a frown. "They might vote to stay."

"You got your way last time, Sam," Cohen replied, "but I don't think you'll be able to sway people this time."

Before the argument escalated further, Mihdí asked Cohen, "Did you say that you have already gotten an offer on the building?"

Before Cohen could answer, Schliebaum piped up, "Yes, when we discussed the possibility of selling the building last year, Charlie Richardson offered us a decent price for it. He's in real estate, with an office just around the corner; it practically backs up to the synagogue, in fact."

"Sounds like someone I should talk to," Mihdí said. "If his office is that close to the synagogue, he may know something about the rabbi's death or even have seen something."

Mihdí got the address of Richardson's office from Abe Cohen. He started to leave when Sam Schliebaum called him back.

"Richardson's office is on the block behind us, Detective," he said. "It'll be faster if you go out the back door. I'm parked in back, off the alley." He walked Mihdí through the office area to the back door and showed him out. "I'm using the space we have back here, which is usually reserved for the rabbi. Jacob mostly walks . . . walked to work, so I have used that spot pretty often." Schliebaum pointed Mihdí through the alley to where Richardson's office was.

The detective walked through the alley to the next street over, where he easily found the office of Richardson Real Estate and Development. The entrance to Richardson's office opened on a long stairway leading up from the street. Mihdí went up and told the receptionist who he was and was ushered into Richardson's office a moment later. Richardson, who looked to be in his late fifties, wore a light green shirt with enough buttons undone to show a white t-shirt underneath. A navy blue blazer hung on a coat tree in the corner of the room. The man was balding but still had enough hair to comb over the bare patches. He stood up and offered his hand to Mihdí as the detective entered.

"I assume you're here about that rabbi's murder, Detective Montgomery," Richardson said after offering Mihdí a seat.

"That's right," Mihdí confirmed. "Did you happen to see or hear anything that might be related to the rabbi's murder in the synagogue?"

"I can tell you absolutely that I saw nothing at all. I came into the office on Tuesday, but I spent the entire afternoon showing a couple around a number of properties in town. I met them at 12:30, and we were out until after 6:00. I dropped them off at their car and didn't come back to the office. First I knew about the murder was when I read the newspaper on Wednesday morning. Tragic, I'd say. He'd actually come up to see me a few times, just to be neighborly, he said. Very polite. I think the congregation liked him."

"Yes, that's what I had heard. Are you part of the congregation, Mr. Richardson?"

"Nope. Not Jewish. Klemme said they had a pretty good-sized congregation over there, but I don't think it included too many Presbyterians."

"Hmm. You might be right about that," Mihdí said with a smile. "Was anyone else in the office that day who might remember something?"

"Ximena, my receptionist, was here, probably from about 10:00 to 5:00. I believe another detective already interviewed her about it. Since we face the other direction, and we both enter the parking lot from Pultney, we wouldn't be likely to see anything, anyway."

"Well, if you think of anything else that might be relevant, please don't hesitate to give me a call. The other matter I wanted to talk to you about is that I understand you have made an offer on the synagogue building."

Richardson frowned. "I made an offer a year ago or whenever the old rabbi left, and I would still honor that offer, but the congregation decided not to sell."

"Has Abe Cohen asked you about it since the rabbi's death?" Mihdí inquired.

"Yup. He was up here not half an hour ago to see if I'd still be interested. I said I'd still be willing to buy the place if it comes to that. But I don't think

Cohen can make that decision by himself; I think it requires a vote by the entire congregation."

Mihdí said, "I understand that's the process. The rabbi's death could cause a few votes to change, I'd think."

"That's quite possible," said Richardson. "It's all the same to me, either way. The synagogue has been here a long, long time. They've certainly been good, quiet neighbors for us as long as we've had our office here. If I were Jewish, I'd certainly come here. For families that live around here, like I do—I live only about a half mile from here—it would be hard to find a more convenient location."

"Good point," said Mihdí. "Thank you for seeing me, Mr. Richardson. Could I ask you for the names and numbers of the couple you showed around on Tuesday? It's routine to follow up."

Richardson picked up a file from his desk, opened it, copied the names and phone number of the couple on a notepad, and handed the sheet to Montgomery. Mihdí thanked him and showed himself out.

* * *

By the time Mihdí emerged from Richardson's office, a light rain had started. Mihdí decided he could use a cup of coffee, so he made his way back through the alley to Kaminer Avenue and ducked into Ahmad Muhammad's Uncommon Brews coffee shop. Mihdí ordered his favorite, a decaf cappuccino, and invited Muhammad to sit down with him to chat.

Mihdí began, "I've been assuming that you are Muslim, Mr. Muhammad, but I shouldn't take that for granted. Am I right?"

Ahmad smiled, "Assuming I'm a Muslim is pretty safe when I'm from Tunisia with a name like mine. It seems as if most Americans also assume I'm a terrorist."

"I apologize for my fellow countrymen, Mr. Muhammad."

The coffee shop owner laughed. "Please call me Ahmad," he said.

"And please call me Mihdí."

"Your name is Mihdí?" Ahmad asked. "Do you also have Islamic background?"

"Only distantly," Mihdí replied. "My mother is Persian, but my family are all Bahá'ís."

"I know very little of Bahá'í," said Ahmad, "although I have heard of it."

"We can talk more about it at some point if you're interested," said Mihdí. "I was wondering about your feelings as a Muslim about having a synagogue next door. Do you have a problem with it?"

"If I did," Ahmad answered, "I wouldn't have opened my store here. We in Tunisia are mostly Arab, with Berber background as well. But in many ways, Tunisians feel more kinship with the West than we do with the Middle East. We don't feel threatened by Israel in the same way that Syria, Lebanon, or Egypt do."

"I see," said Mihdí. "So for you, the Jews next door are just potential customers."

"That's the way I see it," said Ahmad.

"Have you ever detected any prejudice or hostility from the synagogue or its members?"

"No, not a bit. As I said, their rabbi came here often. Other members of their temple come here as well. When they have weekday meetings, they often come here for coffee and snacks, or even for lunch. We always stock some kosher items, and some of them are careful to eat kosher, but not all of them by any means."

"Did you know that the congregation considered selling the building and moving elsewhere last year?" Mihdí asked.

"Yes, I heard about that," Ahmad replied. "I was a bit worried at the time, as they are our neighbors. It wouldn't be good to have another empty building on the block."

"Oh yes, I saw that there were a few empty storefronts," replied Mihdí. "Has it always been that way?"

"It seems like there is always at least one place empty around here," said Ahmad, "but it's been a bit worse lately. There are two empty buildings on this block and two more on the block behind us. I hope it is just a phase and not a trend. No neighbors means less walk-in business. My landlord owns a few of these empty buildings, so I think he's probably anxious to fill them up, too."

"Who owns this building?" Mihdí asked.

"It's owned by the Richardson Agency," replied Ahmad.

"That's Charlie Richardson, just around the corner, right?" Mihdí asked.

"Yes, sir. He's been very good to me over the years."

"Even more reason for him to be concerned about the neighborhood, I guess."

"That's my thought exactly," said Ahmad.

They sipped their coffee in silence for a moment.

"Other than the members of the synagogue," Mihdí inquired, "who are your customers here?"

Ahmad answered immediately, "It's quite a mix. We get some traffic from the public buildings, since we're in the downtown area. The lunch crowd is primarily from the office buildings close by. In the evenings, it's more the single folks who live in the apartments and condos downtown. Oh, and there are lots of young professionals who live in the area that might pick up coffee and a roll on the way to work."

Mihdí was out of coffee and out of questions, so he said good-bye to Ahmad and walked down to Hoffman's Deli, where he spoke again to his friend, Harry Katz. "Do you know if Charlie Richardson owns this building? He seems to own everything else on the block."

"No," Harry said, "I don't think he does." He called to another man to join them. "Neil, this is Detective Mihdí Montgomery, an old friend of mine. Mihdí, this is Neil Hoffman. He owns the place."

Hoffman looked to be about six feet tall, with wavy, dark hair. Mihdí guessed him to be around fifty-five. He wore black pants and a white shirt. He had on what looked like a Rolex watch and was wearing expensive-looking wingtip black shoes. Mihdí asked him about the building.

"I own this building," Hoffman told him. "I guess I'm one of the last holdouts. Richardson and I have talked about me selling it to him, but it's only been talking, nothing serious. If we ever move, I'd certainly go to him first, since he seems to be committed to the area."

"I was talking to Sam Schliebaum and Abe Cohen earlier, and it sounds like there will probably be another vote about moving the synagogue."

"I can't say I'm too surprised," Hoffman said. "It was a close vote a year ago. Sam and I won that one, but I'm sure Abe and friends will use this murder to try to win the vote this time. Abe's been wanting to move for years, but he's had a hard time getting the votes. The cards are stacked against him, you know."

"How so?"

"The people that want to leave, leave. The only ones that are left are those of us who are more inclined to stay." They all laughed. "But Abe might well win this vote, anyway."

"What will you do if the synagogue pulls out?"

"Oh, I expect I'd move, too. I won't let Richardson get this place for less than it's worth, but I think he'll be interested in it. I don't know what he wants it for, though. It's an OK place, but the downtown area isn't really as vibrant a place as it used to be. I suppose he's got big plans for it, though. He always has big plans."

* * *

Mihdí picked up his car from in front of the synagogue and drove to the Area Planning Commission office. Karen Short, one of his neighbors, worked on the staff there. "Do you know anything about Charlie Richardson?" he asked her.

"Oh, yes," she replied at once. "He has a very active real estate agency in town, so we've had dealings with him off and on over the years."

"Has he submitted any major development requests or inquired about zoning changes recently?" Mihdí asked.

"Hmmm," said Karen. "Not that I know of, but I'm not really the one to answer such questions. Why don't you ask my boss, Peter Kowalczyk? He would know if anything were happening."

It turned out that Kowalczyk was available, so Mihdí was able to see him immediately. Kowalczyk appeared to be in his early thirties. He had on suit pants and a tie, but the jacket had been tossed aside and the tie was loosened. He had short-cut blond hair and a well-trimmed moustache. He had an almost blank look on his face, as if perhaps he was left perpetually wondering what was going on. He seemed happy for the distraction of talking to Mihdí, which was giving him an excuse to avoid his work. Mihdí asked him if he

31

knew of any significant zoning appeals, purchases, or development plans from Richardson.

"He doesn't have anything on file with us at the moment," Kowalczyk told him.

"I understand that he made an offer for the Beth Shalom building last year when the congregation was considering selling it," Mihdí said. "Did you know about that at the time?"

"Oh, yes," said Kowalczyk. "Charlie Richardson came in about a year ago and mentioned that it was a possibility. The Village of Pine Bluff has a long-range building plan that includes a downtown revitalization project. Charlie was asking if the block where his office is—and the synagogue, too, now that you mention it—would be eligible for funding to completely redo it into a mixed commercial and residential use area. You know, stores and restaurants on the lower level, with condos above. That's the kind of plan that the village has been considering."

"And would that block be eligible?" Mihdí inquired.

"Depends on the timing and the will of the Village Council, but it could be," said Kowalczyk. "I think the Council is just about ready to move on this. The federal grant for the project is likely to come through soon, possibly as early as next month. When that happens, they'll be looking for available tracts and for partnerships with developers. Charlie's block would be a nice location, but the Council probably won't consider it if it could be tied up in court for years trying to get all the property owners to cooperate. If all the owners were ready to sign on, that would be a different story."

Mihdí thanked Kowalczyk for the information and stopped to chat with Karen Short on his way out. They killed a few minutes catching up before Mihdí looked at his watch and said, "Say, I've got to get going. Andrea has a meeting tonight, and I need to pick up Enoch and Lua."

He retrieved his Mini Cooper from the parking lot and picked up the kids on his way home. Andrea had a dinner date with two of her girlfriends, then she was going directly to a meeting of the Bahá'í Local Spiritual Assembly. Mihdí heated up some leftovers for dinner and added a fresh garden salad. After dinner, he played a game with the two kids, then gave them their baths and got them ready for bed. After three stories, he said it was time for the lights to be out and tucked them in. He sat in Lua's room for a while, just watching her sleep.

It was Mihdí's mother's birthday, so he gave her a call and caught up a bit with her. She lived in a retirement home nearly four hours away, so he wasn't able to visit her as often as she would have liked, but he tried to call at least every couple of weeks. Mihdí's father had died several years earlier. Mihdí's mother, who was almost eighty, had not remarried, but she seemed to have quite a few friends at the retirement home and kept up with other friends by e-mail and phone.

Andrea arrived home about 10:00 p.m. "How was the Assembly meeting, honey?" he asked her.

"It was good," she said, as she gave him a kiss. Andrea was tall at five feet, ten inches and had a large frame to match. She exercised regularly to keep her weight from climbing, but it was a constant struggle. Her skin was very dark, and her hair was black. She changed her hairstyle about once per year, but it was currently straightened and long. She had dark eyes and full lips, and she used no lipstick. Her maroon slacks and matching sweater set were complemented by a heavy gold necklace and large African-themed earrings. Everyone who knew Andrea respected and admired her, but she was usually rather reserved with everyone but Mihdí. He valued her opinions, her ideas, and her support more than anyone else's.

"You'll be happy to hear," she said, "that we're asking Brenda to be the Bahá'í reader for the Interfaith Thanksgiving service next week. I'd better send her an email tonight. Also, we have a little job for you."

"Mmmmm," he replied, thinking that little jobs often seemed to turn out to be major projects.

"Behzad got a call from Newlin Properties yesterday."

"Newlin?" Mihdí asked. "Remind me who that is."

"That's the holding company for the Bluff Village shopping plaza where the Bahá'í Center is," his wife answered.

"Oh, right," said Mihdí. "I knew it sounded familiar, but I couldn't place it."

Andrea continued, "They're in final negotiations with some large con- glomerate to sell the whole strip mall. Apparently, they want to build a combination storefront and condominium complex on the site. When our lease is up in four months, we'll have to vacate."

"That's too bad," Mihdí said. "It's been a good location for us. It's central and the right size. And also the right price."

"That's what we all think, too," his wife replied. "It will take some doing to find another location as good as that one. And we think you're just the guy to do that!"

"So, that's the 'little job,' is it?" Mihdí asked.

"You got it! We thought that with all your connections in town and how much you get around everywhere, you might either know of a place or be able to identify a few possibilities that the Center committee could follow up on. You know the criteria we're looking for: located close to the center of town, in an ethnically diverse neighborhood, affordable, with a big meeting space in addition to smaller classrooms. We don't need you to make arrangements, only to come up with some possibilities. I said you'd be happy to do that."

"You and I may need to have a talk later about volunteering my services," Mihdí said with a pretend frown, "but I think I can do this task. Actually, I was in a perfect place just today. The synagogue would make a great Bahá'í Center, but, of course, it's not available."

"That *would* be a good location," Andrea mused as they headed up to their bedroom and started to get ready for bed. "Jacob's murder won't cause them to want to move and possibly lease their current building, will it?"

Mihdí glanced at Andrea to see if she was joking. "Actually, they've already talked about selling it, and they even have an offer on the table. We don't really have the money to buy a center, do we? We need support from surrounding communities just to afford the rent on our current location."

Andrea nodded as they finished putting on their nightclothes and got into bed. "Yes, that's only a fantasy, I guess. But it would be really cool to transform it into a Bahá'í Center, wouldn't it!"

"It would be great!" Mihdí agreed. "I wonder if a Bahá'í Center there would get the same kind of vandalism as a synagogue?"

"It's not likely we'll ever find out, is it?" Andrea said as they snuggled under the covers.

Friday, Day 3

First thing Friday morning, Captain Sterling sent for Mihdí. When Montgomery arrived in his office, Sterling asked him to close the door and sit down.

"The FBI has been monitoring your progress through me, Mihdí," the captain told him as Mihdí sat down. "I've been feeding them information but also trying to keep them off your back so you can conduct your investigation. But I think they want something pretty concrete the week after Thanksgiving or they're going to take over. They think it's a hate crime, and we really don't have anything that indicates otherwise at this point. They're happy to leave it to us for now, but they have ultimate jurisdiction for hate crimes."

Mihdí shook his head. "Honestly, other than the graffiti, we don't have anything that points one way or the other on that. Nobody saw or heard anything, and there's no physical evidence. At this point, it could have been somebody who just pulled up, entered the synagogue, killed the rabbi, and then left. It's frustrating as can be."

"Yeah, I know," Sterling said. "Where's CSI when you need them, eh? What leads are you currently working on?"

"Actually, I've got several things to follow up on. I need to check on Charlie Richardson's alibi, and I need to speak more with Scott Craig, who discovered the body. His fiancée broke up with him in order to date Rabbi Klemme, so there's some potential for that to be more than just coincidence. I want to meet with the older Sapp boy and find out more about this skinhead connection. Kurt has talked to the other occupants of the block, but I'd like to have a conversation with those I haven't met yet."

35

"Where's your money right now? Still look like the work of an interrupted vandal?"

"I have nothing to go on, but I don't like it. Just a gut feeling so far."

"You mentioned Charlie Richardson. Is that the real estate guy? What's his connection?"

"Two things. His office is right behind the synagogue, so there's the proximity factor. He made an offer on the building about a year ago and says he'll still honor the offer if the congregation wants to sell."

"Any reason to suspect him?" the captain asked.

"Not much, but I suppose if Congregation Beth Shalom were to leave," Mihdí explained, "Richardson would be in a pretty good position to partner with the city on a large redevelopment project. That's thin, but it seems to be at least some kind of motive."

"Check out if he's been talking to anyone on the village council," Sterling said. "A lot of city business is done behind the scenes before things go public. If Richardson is hoping to partner with the city, he'd probably have to be talking to someone at city hall. Try to get the back story on this if you can."

"OK, boss," Mihdí replied as he stood up and turned to leave.

"Montgomery?"

Mihdí turned to look at the captain, still sitting behind his desk.

"You're doing a fine job. Hang in there."

Mihdí gave him a half smile, then walked out the door.

Mihdí wasn't friends with any of the members of the Pine Bluff Village Council, but he did know the Village Clerk pretty well, so he gave her a call later in the morning, after he caught up with his paperwork and e-mail.

"Jill Bartholomew," the voice at the other end answered.

"Jill," said Mihdí, "this is Mihdí Montgomery."

"Great to hear from you, Mihdí," replied Bartholomew. "What can I do for you?"

"I've heard a little about a proposed redevelopment plan," Mihdí said. "Do you know who is talking to whom about it?"

"Just about everybody's talking about it, trying to influence the council," Jill said. "But if you mean who might actually be involved in the project, it basically boils down to three developers: Mark Shipley, Charles Richardson, and Susan Sharp of Southwest Suburban Development. I guess the three of them all have viable proposals. I believe Shipley has two different possibilities he's floating."

"Any scuttlebutt related to these three?" Mihdí inquired.

"Word has it that Sue Sharp is in the best position right now," Jill told him, "but at least some on the council like Richardson's location the best. I believe he is still in the process of finalizing his proposal, so he might yet come out on top."

"That's the block downtown where his office is located?" Mihdí asked.

"That's right," she confirmed. "He has apparently been buying up the properties there for a while because they're close to downtown and easy for him to administer since they're so close by. He's put a good bit of effort into this over the last year or so. His agency used to be just Richardson Real Estate, but he recently added 'Development' to make his offering sound better to the council."

"So he isn't really a big-time developer?"

"Not at all. He really just has a standard real estate agency, although it does have a specialty in commercial properties. But if he gets this deal, it could launch him into the big leagues. Say, is this related to the murder at the synagogue? That's on that block, too, isn't it?"

"I'd rather not start any rumors or speculation," Mihdí said. "Anything else you happen to know about the project?"

"I think I'm out, Detective," she said. "Is there anything else I can do for you?"

"Thanks, Jill, but I think that's it," Mihdí said. "I won't hesitate to call on you if I think you can help."

Mihdí decided it would be a good idea to check in on Charlie Richardson at some point to follow up about the development project. But first he thought it would be worth talking again to Scott Craig, the man who had discovered the rabbi's body, so he called the number he had for him, and Craig picked up on the second ring.

"Scott Craig here," he said. "How can I help you?"

"Hi, Mr. Craig," Mihdí replied. "This is Detective Mihdí Montgomery. I just wanted to follow up with you on some of the things we discussed previously. Is there a convenient time for us to meet today?"

"I'm booked up pretty well until about noon or so," Craig answered. "Would you be able to come here at 1:30?"

"Sure," said Mihdí. "That time will work for me." He made sure he had the address of Craig's office and disconnected.

Mihdí decided he would check in on Andy Sapp. He drove by the Sapp house but found that everyone was gone. So he drove to the high school and checked in at the main office. He waited in the small office the principal offered him while a page went to Andy's classroom and brought him back to the office.

Mihdí had not seen Andy previously, and he would not have recognized him as part of the Sapp family. Andy's father gave the impression of being large and solid, but Andy seemed as wispy as his father seemed sturdy. He was wearing a dark t-shirt with the name of a heavy metal band in dark letters. He had black jeans with no belt. He was also wearing beat-up running shoes with white socks.

Andy looked with barely veiled disgust at the black detective as he was ushered into the room. He slouched down into the office's other chair with his chin on his chest and his eyes fixed firmly on the floor.

"Andy," Mihdí began, "I'm Detective Montgomery of the Pine Bluff Police. I have a few questions I'd like to ask you."

Andy didn't respond in any way.

Mihdí continued, "I have learned that you have some friends that believe that white people are superior to others. Is that correct?"

Andy looked up briefly, then returned his gaze to the floor before answering. "I guess that's one of the things they say," he said.

Mihdí paused a moment before resuming. "For what might be obvious reasons," he finally said, "I don't share that belief."

Andy snorted.

Mihdí ignored the sound and continued, "But really, I don't care that much about what your friends believe. There are lots of people in the world whose beliefs I don't share, and that's to be expected. And I've also noticed over the years that if you check with the members of any group, you'll find that even within the group not all of their beliefs line up. People join groups for different reasons, and knowing that someone is a member of a group doesn't mean you know their beliefs."

Mihdí had been watching Andy carefully as he spoke and could tell that despite the boy's fixed stare at his feet, he was listening to every word. Mihdí laughed, and Andy looked up.

"Sorry for the lecture," he said. "I suspect you must get enough of those from your teachers and your Dad, and don't need another one from me. So, let me get to the point. While I don't care what people believe and not much about what they say, it's very important to me what they do, particularly if it's against the law. What I need to know from you is if this group of friends you're involved with has ever asked you to do anything illegal or if you know of any illegal activities they have organized."

Andy didn't answer for a while. Mihdí waited quietly.

"They've never asked me to do anything illegal," he finally said.

"This would include things like vandalism of a Jewish synagogue or intimidation of Jews, Black people, or others," Mihdí clarified. "They haven't asked you to do anything like that?"

"No," Andy replied firmly.

"And you're not aware of others in the group doing this sort of thing?" Mihdí pressed.

"No," Andy said again.

"Okay," said Mihdí, relaxing back into his chair. "I guess that's okay then. That was really my only concern. I imagine it's pretty nice to find a group where you're accepted for who you are, right?"

"Yeah, that's right," said Andy. "They treat me like an adult there. My opinion matters. They listen to what I have to say."

"Wow, that's terrific," said Mihdí. "You don't have formal meetings, do you?"

"Nah," Andy replied. "We just hang out at somebody's house and talk."

"Sounds great," Mihdí said. "When I was in high school, I had a group of kids I hung out with, too. I never would have made it through high school without my friends. Are there other guys from the high school or is it all older guys?"

"They're all older," Andy said. "But they don't care about my age."

"They're like a bunch of older brothers, huh?"

"Yeah, something like that."

"Do you ever talk about trying to get more guys involved? It might be nice to have some other guys your age."

"I don't care about guys my age," Andy said. "It's not like anybody here in the school cares about me."

"That must be hard," Mihdí said. "It would be really nice to have the guys from your group right there in your classes, wouldn't it? Then you wouldn't have to wait for your weekly group get-togethers."

"We get together more than once a week," Andy scoffed. "I hang out with them lots of times after school."

"Oh, that's even better," Mihdí said. "Once a week would be a long time to wait. How did you meet these guys, since they're not from school? I always felt like I was stuck with friends from school because those were the only guys I ever saw."

"Brent said he saw me a couple of times after school and that I looked more mature than the other kids. Eventually, he asked me if I wanted to come to his house and hang out."

"This is Brent Wiegand we're talking about?" Mihdí asked, making a connection with the name that Darla Brownlee had mentioned for the skinhead recruiter.

"That's right," answered Andy. "How did you know that?"

"Somebody else mentioned his name to me just yesterday in a completely different context," Mihdí said. "So you and Brent sort of hit it off immediately? He probably remembered his own high school years and could tell you were a kindred spirit. Did he go to your high school when he was younger?"

"Yeah," said Andy. "It wasn't that long ago. I don't know exactly how old he is, but he's not that much older than I am."

"Is Brent kinda like the leader of the group?"

"Yeah," Andy said. "Seems like we're always doing whatever he comes up with."

"You ever play basketball or anything like that?" Mihdí asked.

"Nah, we're not into sports."

"Do any of the guys play in bands or anything?"

"Sometimes we play a little bit," Andy replied. "Damon and I both play guitar, and Dylan has drums, so we've jammed a little a couple of times. Brent's not really that into it, so it's only been a couple of times."

"Sounds like you might want to do that a bit more?" Mihdí queried.

Andy nodded. "Maybe," he said.

"There's a group of guys that get together down at the community center on Saturday mornings. One of their guitarists moved away a few months ago. They might be really happy if you brought your guitar over there now and then and played with them. Wouldn't have to be any commitment, of course, since you already have your own friends. But it might be fun for you now and then. I actually have gone down there and played with them myself a couple of times. But I'm more of an acoustic guitarist, and they're all electric."

"You play guitar?" Andy asked.

"Oh, yeah," Mihdí replied. "I've been playing since I was about twelve. Don't have much time for it now, because I have a couple of young kids. But I wasn't too bad back in college. I played in a band back then, and we did a couple of gigs."

Andy looked at Mihdí with more curiosity now and had dropped the antagonism.

"Well," said Mihdí. "I should let you go. I've been yakking away long after I found out all I needed to know. I just don't get much chance to talk to interesting kids, so it's been a nice treat. Thanks for indulging me. It's been a real pleasure to meet you."

He shook Andy's hand and put an arm around his shoulder as he ushered him out of the small room. He smiled as Andy left the office area to return to class.

Mihdí returned to his car and made some notes of what he had learned about the group that Andy had been hanging out with. He called Darla Brownlee to give her the names of the people involved: Brent Wiegand, Damon, and Dylan. She promised she'd look into it, although she commented that it didn't sound like a very serious threat once he had described the group to her.

* * *

After his talk with Andy Sapp, Mihdí drove back to Kaminer Avenue and parked a few buildings south of the synagogue, near Hoffman's Deli. He looked around a bit and checked some of the notes that Kurt Childs had written up about his initial inquiries on the block. He decided to drop in on the HisStory Christian Bookstore.

Mihdí identified himself to the young man working there and said, "I see from your nametag that your name is Matthew. Do you mind if I ask you a few questions?"

"I guess not," said Matthew.

"May I ask your surname, Matthew?" Mihdí began.

"You don't have to call me sir."

"I . . . what? Oh, no, I just wanted your last name."

"Skefton," Matthew replied. He spelled it, "S – K – E – F – T – O – N."

Mihdí observed the young man as he made a show of writing down his name. He judged Skefton to be in his early twenties. His blond hair was cut short over his entire scalp. He had no facial hair. He wore a maroon long-sleeved polo shirt with the HisStory Christian Bookstore logo on it, and Mihdí suspected this was a required uniform for the staff. Skefton was also wearing black jeans, black socks, and black athletic shoes. He gave off a very odd vibe, as if he were expecting to be attacked somehow and was working to fend it off in advance. He looked at Mihdí only in passing and never met his eyes.

"I understand that you were working here last Tuesday," Mihdí stated. "Is that correct?"

"Yeah," Matthew said.

"I imagine Detective Childs already asked you if you had seen or heard anything suspicious on that day, particularly in the afternoon?"

"Yeah, some guy interviewed me," Skefton said. "I told him I didn't see nothin' unusual."

"Was it busy that day?" the detective asked.

"I don' think so," said Skefton. "We had a few customers that day, I think, but nothing much."

"Would you have a record of any sales made that day?"

"I don't," Matthew said. "Mebbe Mrs. Plante's got somethin'."

"That's the owner, I suppose," Mihdí inquired.

"Yeah," Matthew replied. "Her number's here on this card. She'll probably be in about noon. She usually comes in for an hour or so so's I can have my lunch."

"Is that right?" Mihdí asked. "Did she do that last Tuesday?"

"I don't really remember that day," said Matthew, "but I probably would remember if she hadn't come in, since that would have required some special arrangements."

"Great," said Mihdí, "I'll check with her about what she remembers from that day. Did you know Rabbi Klemme yourself? I understand he came in here from time to time."

"Yeah, I knew who he was," Matthew said, frowning slightly. "I . . ." He left the sentence uncompleted.

"You were going to say something?" Mihdí asked. He could sense a change in Skefton's attitude since he mentioned the rabbi.

"Nah. I got nothin' more to say."

"Do you happen to remember if Rabbi Klemme came into the store that day?"

"No, he didn't. I would remember that."

"When was the last time you remember seeing him?" Mihdí pursued.

"Dunno. Maybe last week sometime."

"How do you feel about having a synagogue so near the bookstore?"

Matthew scowled. "I'd like to see it turned into a real church. I'm not really comfortable with those people."

Mihdí felt the depth of the young man's anti-Semitism and it made him angry, but he pushed the feeling down. "Did the rabbi ever buy books here?"

"What would a Jew want with Christian books?" Matthew scoffed.

"The two religions are very closely related, as I'm sure you know," Mihdí offered. "What you call the Old Testament is the Jewish holy scripture."

"I don't know nothin' about that," Matthew retorted. "I just try to do what Jesus would do."

"And you think He would want you to shun the Jews?" Mihdí asked him, incredulously.

"I said I don't know nothin' about all that. Just leave me alone, OK?"

43

"Where did you take your lunch last Tuesday?"

"I bring my lunch, so I go into the back and study the Bible while I'm eatin' it."

"Is there a back door?" Mihdí said.

"Of course there is," Matthew said, his face flushing red with anger. "Are you sayin' that I killed him?"

"I try to keep an open mind," Mihdí said. Something about Skefton made Mihdí want to push him to see how he would react. "I need to investigate all the possibilities and ascertain the facts."

"Well, I'm glad he's dead!" Skefton said. "I didn't like him. But I didn't kill him. 'Thou shalt not kill,' remember?"

This pushed Mihdí right over the edge. "Oh, I remember," he said coldly. "The Ten Commandments are a very important basis of *Jewish* law. Of course, according to your namesake, St. Matthew, Jesus said, 'Thou shalt love thy neighbor as thyself.' I personally feel that 'neighbor' includes all humanity, not just Christians."

"I didn't kill him, and I don't need to answer your stupid questions," Matthew said.

"Thanks for your time, Mr. Skefton," Mihdí said. "I'll be in touch if I need anything further."

"Don't bother!" Skefton said. He sat down behind the counter, picked up his Bible and began to read.

Mihdí left the shop and went to his car. As soon as he sat down, he began to feel bad about having baited the young man. He felt a need to apologize for getting into a religious argument with someone who was obviously very committed to his beliefs. So, he gave himself another few minutes to calm down, then got up and returned to the store. Matthew started to get up when he heard the door but sat back down when he saw who it was. Mihdí proceeded to the counter and waited until Matthew looked up at him.

"I want to apologize for arguing with you," Mihdí said. "It was rude and uncalled-for. I'm sorry."

Matthew sat silent for a few moments, then gave a quick nod. "It's OK," he said.

"It's not OK," said Mihdí, "but can I take it that you accept my apology?" Matthew nodded again.

"Thank you," said Mihdí. "I hope you have a good day."

He turned and left the shop. He got in his car again, took out Mrs. Plante's card and punched in her number on his cell phone. Her full name, he noticed, was Stephanie Plante. After four rings, her voice mail kicked in. Mihdí left his name and number and asked her to call him back.

* * *

Mihdí felt that he could take a little time to talk to a realtor friend about the possibilities for a Bahá'í Center. He dropped in on his friend Erica Iyer at Gewirtz Realty.

"Hello, Mihdí!" she exclaimed. "It has been so long since I have seen you. How have you been? How are Andrea and the kids? Are you still living in that lovely house on Spitznagle? What can I do for you?"

Mihdí laughed at the multiple questions. "I'm fine, Andrea and the kids are fine, and we're still living on Spitznagle. How are Bala and your kids?"

"We are all fine, too, Mihdí," she replied with a laugh. Erica Iyer was five foot four with long, dark brown hair. Mihdí knew from experience that she was a gourmet Indian cook, and she sported the extra weight that proved how irresistible her cooking was. As usual, she wore a brightly-colored suit and coordinated blouse. She had a personality that was constantly upbeat, and she always wore a smile.

"And how's the real estate business these days?" Mihdí asked.

"It seems that it is possibly picking up a bit lately," she said. "It's been slow for the last couple of years, but we've had a slight bump over the last two or three months. I hope it is a trend and not just a short-term flash."

"Yes," Mihdí replied, "it would be nice if the whole economy could come together again."

"O Lord, hear our prayer!" Erica said, raising her arms in mock supplication. They both laughed.

"I wonder if you would help me with a little project, Erica," Mihdí said.

"If I can," she replied.

"The local Bahá'í community is going to be losing its center in a few months," he started.

"The one in Bluff Village?" Iyer asked. "Oh, that's where Newlin is going to develop the new multiuse facility, isn't it?"

"That's right," Mihdí answered. "They don't plan to renew our lease when it's up in four months. So, we need to find a new place. We need something not far from downtown that has a big meeting room as well as some smaller rooms for children's classes and things like that. And we don't have a big budget, either."

"Hmm," Erica mused. "There's certainly some possibilities in town, but this isn't a very good time for it."

"Even with the economy down?" Mihdí asked. "I'd think people would be eager to find tenants just now."

"Well, they will be in a few months, but there's this big downtown redevelopment project coming up. There's three or four developers who are hoping to partner with the city on it. They've been buying up key properties and holding off on getting new tenants so they'll have more complete packages to offer the city. The city can exercise eminent domain over a few properties, but they won't want to do it with too many because it ticks . . . it upsets people. The developers want to present their options with as few problem cases as possible."

"Oh, I see," Mihdí said. "This project is keeping some empty properties off the market right now. And when the council reviews the developer's proposals and chooses one as the site for the redevelopment, the other sites will no longer need to be held and they'll be made available again."

"Exactly," his friend said. "Once that all happens, there could be some good bargains to be had."

Mihdí felt his cell phone vibrate in his pocket. He quickly pulled it out and checked it. The display showed that Stephanie Plante was calling him. He decided to let his voicemail pick it up. Putting the phone back into his pocket and glancing up at Erica again, he asked, "Any idea of the timing of all this? You don't think it will be settled in time for us to move in March or so?"

"I doubt it," she replied. "The Village Council probably wants to move fast, but a big process like this will have to be written up, and there will have to be plenty of time for accepting bids and probably for public comment. I'm not sure if an environmental impact assessment will have to be done for this, but it wouldn't surprise me. Even if everything goes very smoothly, it probably wouldn't all be settled until sometime in the summer."

"Well, that's going to be a big problem for the Baháʼís," Mihdí said. "Maybe we'll have to do without a center for a while. We've got so much going on there, I'm not sure how that would even work."

"You should talk to Newlin," Erica offered. "They probably feel obliged to end your lease when it's up, but they're not likely to be quite ready to start demolition in April. You may be able to get a month by month extension until they're actually ready to start the project."

"Good thinking," Mihdí said. "Please keep your eyes and ears open for good properties for us, but I'll suggest to the Center committee that they talk to Newlin as well. Give my regards to Bala."

"And mine to Andrea," Erica replied.

* * *

As soon as he had stepped out the door of Gewirtz Realty, Mihdí called Stephanie Plante back. She picked up and told him that she was coming to the HisStory Book Store, and they arranged for him to meet her there. He drove back over to that neighborhood and found a spot to park near the bookstore. When he entered the bookstore, Plante had not yet arrived, so Matthew was still behind the counter.

Sensitive to the discomfort he had caused Matthew earlier, Mihdí said, "I'm meeting Ms. Plante here in a few moments, but I'll wait outside." He stepped back outside and paced up the sidewalk a bit. He waved at Ahmad Muhammad through the window of the coffee shop, but he didn't go inside.

Stephanie Plante stepped out of the bookstore just a few minutes later. "Sorry, I came in the back door. Matthew said you were out here. Please come in."

As Mihdí walked into the store with Stephanie Plante, Matthew exited, on his way to lunch.

"Matthew usually stays here for his lunch and eats in the back room," Stephanie said once they were inside. "He said that since you were here, he didn't want to be around. I guess you and he didn't exactly bond?"

Mihdí smiled. "I think that's an accurate statement. I suspect I pushed some of his buttons; I know he pushed mine."

Plante raised an eyebrow quizzically, but Mihdí did not elaborate.

Stephanie Plante looked every inch a businesswoman. She wore a conservative forest green wool business suit with a skirt that fell below her knees. She had a lighter green mock turtleneck underneath and a necklace with a small plain gold cross that hung just below her turtleneck's collar. Her light brown hair was cut relatively short, with a strong wave throughout and no bangs. Her nails were perfectly shaped but had no signs of polish. She walked with an air of total self-assurance.

"I gather you're the owner of this store," Mihdí began.

"Yes," she answered, "with my husband. We own both this store and the original HisStory location in the Loop."

"Matthew told me that you were probably here last Tuesday, the day of the murder at the synagogue."

"Probably?" she asked.

"Well," said Mihdí, "he thought he would have remembered if you hadn't been here, but couldn't say for sure that you were."

She smiled, "OK, that explains that. Yes, I was here that day. It's a terrible thing that happened. Jacob came in often, both to shop and just to visit."

"Often?" Mihdí asked. "Matthew seemed to indicate that his visits were pretty rare."

"Mmm," she mused. "Matthew didn't like him very much, and Jacob didn't want to upset him. He most often stopped by when I was here."

"That makes sense," Mihdí said. "Why didn't Matthew like him?"

"I assume you asked him that already," Stephanie said, "but it was because of Matthew's religious beliefs. He feels that his flavor of Christianity is the only right road. He is judgmental enough about other brands of Christians, but he seems to have a special disgust for Jews."

"What's that about, do you think?" Mihdí asked.

"His church teaches that Jews were the chosen ones of God," she explained. "They believe that God gave them a special one-time chance to recognize Christ. Now they believe that Christians are the chosen people and that the long suffering of the Jewish people is punishment for rejecting Jesus."

"I've heard that before," Mihdí said quietly. "It's very disturbing to me, I have to say. And I'm saying that personally, not as a police officer."

"Actually, I have trouble with it, too," Stephanie replied. "I keep hoping that being exposed to good people of all persuasions here in the store will help him to realize that his church doesn't have a monopoly on truth."

"Doesn't seem to be working," Mihdí observed.

"No," she answered, "I guess it's not. But if he can't get a break from me, who will he ever get one from? And he's been a very reliable employee. In the . . . what, maybe four months he's been working here, I don't even know of him having been late. I gave him his own keys after he'd been here about a month because he had shown himself to be completely trustworthy by that time."

Mihdí nodded. "It's a good thing you're doing, and I wish you luck with it. I have to ask you some other questions, though."

"Shoot," she said.

"Do you remember what time you were here last Tuesday?" he asked.

"I usually get here between 11:30 and noon," she said. "I don't remember that day being different, but let me check my calendar." She got her iPhone from her purse behind the counter and manipulated it for a few moments.

"Oh, that was the day the rep from Thomas Nelson was up from Nashville," she said. "I met with him at our downtown store in the morning, and I got a bit of a late start out here. I didn't arrive until about 2:00."

"And Matthew was here at that point?" Mihdí asked.

"Yes, I called him before I left the store and told him when I'd be here. He told me it was no problem holding off on his lunch break until then. I stayed until just before 3:30."

"Do you remember what he did when you arrived?"

"We chatted for a few minutes as we usually do, then he went in the back to eat his lunch."

49

"Did he stay there the entire time you were here? I know there's a back door. Did you go back there while you were working? Any chance he slipped out for a while?"

"I went back there a few times to check on special orders, but customers kept me out front most of the time. And the lunch area is sheltered a bit, so even if I had gone back there, I wouldn't have known for sure that he was there. He usually just reads quietly while he's eating and after he finishes."

"Have you ever known of him going out?"

"Oh, sure. Sometimes he'll run an errand during lunch or just go out for a walk or some fresh air. He doesn't smoke, so he doesn't have to go out all the time, but it certainly happens."

"And there's no alarm or bell or anything that says that the back door is being opened?"

"No, nothing like that. We have a buzzer so people making deliveries can get our attention, but Matthew has a key, so he wouldn't use that."

Mihdí had made a few notes as she was talking. "I want to ask for your personal opinion now," he said. "I imagine that you, as a businesswoman, have to make judgments about people often. But I also imagine that as a good-hearted Christian, you sometimes find your judgment befogged a bit by your love for humanity and seeing God in them."

"That's a lovely way to think of it," she said.

"But to the extent possible," he continued, "I'd like you to set that part aside and give me your coldest opinion. Do you think that Matthew—because of the depths of his beliefs—would be capable of murdering Rabbi Klemme?"

She closed her eyes, and a pained expression crossed her face. "I don't like to think that anyone is capable of murder," she said at last, "least of all someone I know personally. But I know that some people do kill others. And I know how difficult it is for Matthew to accept the possibility that people could hold different beliefs than those he does. He has a very hard time holding his tongue when someone buys a book that he doesn't like. I occasionally find books not put out on the shelf when they have titles or content he finds objectionable. That's all to say how deep his commitment is to what he holds dear.

"Based on that, I'd have to say that it just might be possible for him to commit murder, if he thought that it was somehow doing God's will. He has mentioned several times that if the Jews would just move out, the synagogue could be cleansed and become a Christian church. Perhaps he even thinks Faith Tabernacle would want to expand into it."

They were both silent for a few moments.

"That's so creepy," she said, "just to contemplate the possibility that he could have killed someone."

"I can certainly understand that," Mihdí replied. "As you said earlier, it's difficult to swallow that anyone could ever be capable of murder, yet we know it happens. In this case, though, I need you to forget the idea as completely as you can for now. Matthew seems troubled to me, and he needs the love and help that you have given him here. I have no evidence at all—none—that he was involved in the rabbi's murder. The fact that there is a remote chance that he could have done it means that I have something more that must be investigated, but it certainly does not convict him. It doesn't even point a finger at him. So, please, just continue to think of him as Matthew, a strong and devoted Christian who wants to see God's will working in the world."

Stephanie smiled and nodded. "Of course, that's the right thing to do," she said. "I'll do my best not to let possibility turn into probability."

"I'm afraid I have another question for you," Mihdí said. "Can you verify that you were here in the store the entire time that you were in this area? Do you have witnesses that saw you here? And can you verify that you left the area after you left the store?"

"Well," she said, "that puts a different spin on the whole idea of suspicion, doesn't it? Let me look at the cash register records."

She unlocked a filing cabinet just inside the back area and took out the sales records. She found the ones from Tuesday.

"Oh, yes," she said, "here are the names of a few customers that were in that day." She wrote down a few names and phone numbers from her records and gave them to Mihdí. "They actually all overlapped, I think, so they should provide a pretty good account that I was here in the store the entire time. And I stopped in to get a coffee from Mr. Muhammad next door as I was leaving. No, wait, it was Mr. Muhammad's nephew—Azam, or something like that. He may or may not be able to verify the time. But I said something to him about how late I was returning downtown, so he might remember. And I went straight back to the Chicago store, which didn't take long at that time of day, so it wouldn't leave too many minutes unaccounted for."

"Thanks for that," Mihdí said. "Sounds like you would make a lousy suspect, but I have to consider all possibilities."

"I understand," Plante said. "Best of luck in your investigation."

"Thank you very much," Mihdí said. "I'll keep both of you in my prayers."

* * *

Mihdí left HisStory and walked down to Hoffman's deli. It was a bit after noon by that time, so he decided to get some lunch. Harry Katz didn't seem to be working, and Mihdí didn't see Neil Hoffman, either. He ordered a corned beef sandwich with potato salad and chatted with the worker who was preparing it for him. When he went to find a seat, he saw an old friend at one of the tables and asked to join her. He took a break from his investigation to catch up with his friend. They talked for about an hour, until Mihdí had to leave in order to meet Scott Craig.

Craig's office was not actually in Pine Bluff but was located two suburbs over. The traffic had not started picking up for the day yet, though, so Mihdí made good time. He got to the right building and entered. There was a directory that showed that Craig's office was on the fifth floor, so Mihdí took the elevator up. The receptionist's desk was empty when he arrived, but there was a bell on the desk. A woman in jeans and a loose-fitting Chicago Bears sweatshirt came out through a secured door in answer to his ring.

Mihdí pointed to her sweatshirt and said, "The Bears didn't do so well on Sunday, did they?"

The lady sighed. "It's been a long season already," she said, "and they're just not improving. But they still have a chance against Kansas City next week."

"Anything could happen," Mihdí offered.

"What can I do you for?" the lady asked.

"I have an appointment with Scott Craig at 1:30," he said.

"I think Scott has left for the day," she said. "Hang on a second while I go check."

She went back through into the main part of the office, using her key card. She was only gone about two minutes. "His secretary said Scott wasn't feeling very well and went home at lunchtime," she said when she returned.

"Hmm," Mihdí said. "I guess he forgot to write down our appointment or didn't feel up to giving me a call. It's no big deal. I'll catch up with him later, I guess. Thanks for your time."

"No problem," the lady said. "Sorry you came for nothing."

"Not for nothing," he said. "I got a hot tip on the Bears game!"

They were both laughing as Mihdí left to make his way back down to his car. The detective did not rule out the possibility that Craig was actually feeling ill but thought it was more likely that Craig's absence indicated he was avoiding Mihdí for some reason. Mihdí didn't think Craig was a flight risk. He decided that if Craig was worried about something he'd let him worry for another day, and if Craig was truly ill, the detective would give him a day to recover.

* * *

Mihdí checked with dispatch to get a number for Faith Tabernacle, which turned out to be in Romeoville. He called the number and got an answering machine that said the pastor, Rev. Elijah Crestwood, would return his call. He left a message with his name and number, saying that it was a police matter.

Charlie Richardson's alibi was a couple that he had escorted around Pine Bluff to look at houses on Tuesday. Since Richardson himself had supplied their name and number, Mihdí decided it wouldn't hurt to talk to them. He called the number that Richardson had given him. It turned out that the couple, Barry and Meredith Grant, lived in Des Plaines. They said they would be home, and Mihdí felt that he might as well make a trip up there. While a phone call might suffice, he thought that meeting them in person might provide more information than he could get over the phone. Plus, he never minded spending time in his Mini.

53

The drive took him about forty-five minutes, so he arrived at the Grants' house a bit after 2:30 p.m. When he rang the doorbell, a young white man with neatly trimmed red hair came to the door carrying a small child who was perhaps a year old and a shade or two darker than her father. Mihdí showed his badge and identified himself and was ushered into the house. A young black woman joined them from the kitchen. Both she and the young white man were dressed in jeans and t-shirts. There were some boxes around the walls—mostly empty—but a few were already packed.

"You are Barry and Meredith Grant?" Mihdí asked.

They nodded.

"I'm investigating a crime in Pine Bluff," Mihdí continued. "I understand that you were in the area last Tuesday, looking at houses."

"Yes, sir," said Barry Grant. "We spent all afternoon there. Say, we're both beat from a day of packing and wouldn't mind sitting down. Come on into the living room. Can I get you a Coke or something?"

"No, nothing for me, thanks. I won't be long." Mihdí came with them to the living room and took a seat. "Can you confirm that Charlie Richardson was with you without a break from about 12:30 p.m. until 6:00 p.m.?"

"That's right," Barry said. "We met him at a shopping center in the north part of town, which turned out to be very close to the first property we went to see. We went in his car for the rest of the day until he returned us to our car a few minutes after 6:00. I think we saw twelve houses."

"So you're considering buying a house in Pine Bluff?" Mihdí inquired.

"Absolutely," Barry said. "I'm starting a job down there after the new year, and it's too long a commute from here. We actually saw two houses that we might be interested in, so we're planning to go down next Wednesday morning for another look. We're hoping to look at a few other houses first, then revisit the two we liked."

"Did you have your child along with you last Tuesday? I don't remember Richardson mentioning that, although it might have slipped his mind."

"No, no, no, no, no," Meredith Grant replied with a smile. "We left Chelsea with Barry's mother here in Des Plaines while we looked at houses. Chelsea would never have made it through a whole afternoon of house-shopping. We're going to leave her there again next week when we go back to Pine Bluff."

"Sounds like a good choice," Mihdí replied with a smile. "Did Mr. Richardson talk about his business at all while you were with him?"

"It depends on what you mean by that," Meredith said. "He talked about real estate the entire time. He told us stories about terrible and special houses he had seen. He talked about the school system down there, too. That's one of the reasons we chose Pine Bluff, because we had heard they have exceptional schools there. Charlie confirmed that for us. He said his own kids attend Bluff Point Elementary and that he loves the teachers there. One of the houses we especially liked is in the Bluff Point school area. But he said all the schools are pretty good."

"That's my impression, too," Mihdí said. "My son goes to Abbott Elementary, and I certainly am happy with the staff there."

"That's further south, right?" Barry asked. "We didn't see anything in that area that really turned us on."

"Well, I hope you can find something that's perfect," Mihdí said. "I'd better start heading back towards home. The traffic will only get worse as it gets later."

* * *

Mihdí decided his next step would be to talk to Brent Wiegand. He got back to Pine Bluff at about 3:45 and drove to the address for Wiegand that Darla Brownlee had in her files. Mihdí noted that Wiegand's apartment was just a few blocks from the high school that Andy Sapp attended.

A pale, thin young man answered the door when Mihdí rang the bell. The man kept the security chain fastened and peered through the crack. "What do you want?" he asked.

"I'm Detective Mihdí Montgomery of the Pine Bluff Police," Mihdí replied, showing his badge. "I am investigating the involvement of one of your friends in criminal activity and I would like to talk to you about him."

"What friend?" Wiegand asked.

"Andy Sapp," Mihdí said. "May I come in?"

Wiegand closed the door, released the security chain, and reopened it to let Mihdí enter.

"What's Andy done?" Wiegand asked, as soon as Mihdí was in the room. Brent Wiegand was probably five foot ten and very thin. His skin had the pallid tone of someone who rarely spent time outside. He had prominent tattoos on both sides of his neck, as well as some down each arm, all the way to the wrists. His left eyebrow and his nose were both pierced. When he spoke, it turned out that his tongue was also pierced. He wore a dark t-shirt and black pants. He was barefoot. The television was blaring in the corner of the room, and there was an open beer bottle on a low table next to a ratty couch.

"That has yet to be determined," the detective replied. "There's been a murder and some vandalism, and I need to find out whether Andy is involved and how. Do you know anything about the crime at Beth Shalom synagogue, Mr. Wiegand?"

"Are you asking about me or about Andy?" Wiegand asked, suspiciously.

"Well, obviously anything you know would be relevant," Mihdí said. "I've talked to Andy about it, and he mentioned that he spends a lot of time with you, so I wanted to see if you knew anything about it."

"I don't know a thing," Wiegand said. "I saw it on the news, but I don't know nuthin."

"In any of your conversations with Andy," Mihdí persisted, "has he mentioned any criminal activity that he's been involved in or was contemplating?"

"If he did, I sure as hell wouldn't tell you about it, would I?" Wiegand said. "Some friend I'd be if I ratted on my own buddies."

Mihdí hadn't expected to get any information about illegal activity from Wiegand, but had mostly wanted to put him on notice that the police had an eye on him.

"Andy had some anti-Black flyers at his home that he said he had gotten from you."

"There's no crime against flyers, is there?" Wiegand said. "I got freedom of speech."

"For many people it seems to be a short step from racist beliefs to discriminatory or even violent action," Mihdí said. "While there's no law against expressing your views, there are laws against putting some of them into action."

"Well, I ain't done that," Wiegand stated, "and neither has Andy. Is that it?"

"Sorry, no," said the detective, "I need to ask where you were on Tuesday afternoon."

"I was at work until 3:00 p.m., then I took the bus home. It gets to my block about twenty minutes or a quarter to 4:00, just like today. I got to the house no more than two minutes before you did."

"Can anyone verify that information for Tuesday?" Mihdí asked.

"You can check my timecard if you want," Wiegand snapped back.

"Could anyone on the bus confirm that you rode it on Tuesday?"

"How would I know? I don't talk to people on the bus. I wouldn't be able to pick any other passengers out of a lineup. How would they be able to confirm I was there on some particular day? Are we done?"

"Yes, thank you, that's all for now," Mihdí said. "I'll be in touch if I have further questions."

"You do that, police dude," Wiegand responded. He got up as Mihdí opened the door to leave and slammed the door behind the detective.

Mihdí couldn't help but chuckling to himself. Over the years, he had found that most of what he learned about people came from the way they reacted rather than what they actually said. He returned to his office, passed Stephanie Plante's list of customers to Kurt Childs, and asked him to check with them. He then called Beth Carr to see if she had turned up anything new in processing the evidence from the synagogue, but she had nothing to report. After speaking with Officer Carr, he completed his paperwork for the day and headed for home.

Mihdí picked up the kids on his way home from work, and they each found something to play with in the living room while Mihdí broiled some salmon and cut up and steamed some broccoli to go with it. He heated up some leftover rice in the microwave. Andrea came home from a workout just as he was placing dinner on the table. While they were eating, the children told their parents about their day at school. Lua had discovered the day before that one of her front teeth was a little loose, and she was very excited about the prospect of losing her very first tooth. Andrea and Mihdí took turns wiggling it and expressing their congratulations to their youngest.

They were just finishing up dinner at about 6:30 when Mihdí got a call on his cell phone that turned out to be Rev. Elijah Crestwood from Faith

Tabernacle. Mihdí excused himself to the study to talk.

"Sorry I didn't return your call earlier," Rev. Crestwood said. "I work a regular job during the week, and I only just got home."

"That's no problem," Mihdí told him. "Do you have a few minutes now that I can ask you some questions?"

"Yes, sir," the minister said.

"Do you know a young man named Matthew Skefton?" Mihdí asked him. "I believe he's a member of your congregation."

"Yes, of course I know Matthew," the pastor replied. "He's one of my most faithful members. Is he in trouble of some sort?"

"Would that surprise you?" Mihdí inquired. He didn't particularly want to give the pastor any information until he had gotten some answers.

Crestwood didn't reply immediately. After a short pause, he said, "You haven't told me if he's in trouble. If he is, I would like to know so I can help him. He's like a son to me."

Rather than face the minister's concern head-on, Mihdí tried once again to ignore the question, "Could you please describe Matthew to me in your own words? And I'm not talking about physical description, but character and temperament and such."

"Listen, Mr. Detective," the minister said. "I have asked you twice if Matthew is in trouble, and you have not told me. I want to know what's going on."

"I appreciate your concern, Rev. Crestwood," Mihdí replied, resigned to the fact that he could no longer brush the pastor's concerns aside, "but I'm afraid I need you to answer my questions before I answer yours. If you cooperate, I will tell you what I can about the situation. If not, I won't tell you anything. Are you ready to cooperate now?"

"You don't seem to be leaving me much choice. Ask your questions."

"Please describe Matthew Skefton for me, if you would," Mihdí asked.

"Matthew is a very dedicated Christian," the pastor stated. "I haven't known him all that long, but he reads the Bible daily and works at applying its lessons to his life. There is nothing he wouldn't do for Jesus. And there's nothing he wouldn't do for the sake of his church, either. I wish I had more parishioners who are so committed to what we're trying to do at Faith Tabernacle."

"And what are you trying to do, exactly?"

"We're carrying out the Great Commission, Mr. Montgomery."

"As in, 'Go therefore and make disciples of all nations . . .'?"

"I teach the King James version," the minister said, "'Go ye therefore, and teach all nations, baptizing them in the name of the Father, and of the Son, and of the Holy Ghost . . .'"

"Same thing," Mihdí ventured. "One translation is as good as another."

"No, they're not as good," the pastor replied. "God inspired the translators of the King James Version, and that is why it has endured for so many years while the others pass in and out of favor."

"If Matthew felt it was God's will that he kill someone, do you think he would do it?" Mihdí asked.

"Of course not," the minister replied. "God said, 'Thou shalt not kill.' That's a commandment, not a suggestion."

"So you do not believe in war or capital punishment, then?"

"Don't play games with me, Detective," the minister snapped. "Ask your questions and tell me what's going on."

"You're right," Mihdí said. "I apologize. That was out of line. How long has Matthew been a part of your church?"

Crestwood paused for a few moments. "Well, let's see. He came to me maybe four or five months ago. He had gotten into a little bit of trouble, and they had suggested that he might want to find a church."

"They?" Mihdí questioned. "A judge suggested he find a church?"

"Oh, no," the pastor replied. "Matthew never went to court. It was just a matter of tagging—you know, like graffiti—on a building. He got caught in the act. His case was diverted to the Victim-Offender Reconciliation Program. A mediator worked with him and the victim to try to reconcile them without Matthew having to get a criminal record. Matthew has told me this story a few times, so I know the details. He had to clean off the graffiti as well as he could, then repaint that side of the building. Oh, and apologize, of course."

"I'm aware of VORP's work through my wife," Mihdí said. "Was that in Romeoville?"

"No, I believe it was in Joliet. But since Matthew is from this area, I believe he worked with a VORP representative from Pine Bluff. It was actually a young rabbi from there. I can't remember his name, but I met him at the time."

"Jacob Klemme, by any chance?" asked Mihdí.

"That's the one," Rev. Crestwood confirmed. "Do you know him?"

"My wife told me she had met him through VORP, but of course she didn't know about the connection with Matthew. So, Rabbi Klemme suggested that Matthew find a church?"

"That's right. A bit odd, wouldn't you say? But that's what happened. Somebody Matthew's mother knew referred him to Faith Tabernacle. The first time he came to meet me here, Rabbi Klemme came along, probably just to make sure Matthew actually showed up. I took a liking to the boy, and he seemed to sincerely want to turn his life around. He started coming to church and almost immediately gave his life to the Lord. Since then he has attended church regularly, as well as Bible study and other activities. He doesn't have lots of friends in the church, as far as I can tell, and just goes it alone, I guess."

Mihdí took a moment to absorb that information. "You say Matthew talked about himself some. Did he tell you how he felt about having been led to the church by a Jew?"

"Actually, he did talk about that a fair bit," Crestwood acknowledged. "It really bothered him, to be honest. Somehow, it didn't seem right to him."

"What does your church teach about members of the Jewish faith?" Mihdí asked.

"Jews are lost creatures," Crestwood said. "They were God's chosen people before the coming of Christ the Lord. They had their chance to accept him as the Messiah. Those who did and became followers of Jesus Christ are counted among the saved. Those that did not are now wandering outside the path of God. But they are certainly not alone in that, and they are not beyond the hope of salvation."

"So do you think this teaching contributed to Matthew's unease?"

"I'm sure it did. It's not like being brought to God by Satan or anything like that, but why would someone who lives in darkness encourage you to turn on a light?"

"What's your explanation for that?" Mihdí asked.

"For me, I like to see the hand of God in everything that happens, good or bad. In this case, the rabbi may not have any idea why he said what he said, but I feel that God put the words into his mouth in order to bring Matthew to salvation."

"Interesting theory . . ." Mihdí said. "Did Matthew say more about this subject?"

"Well, as I said, it bothered him a lot. He'd try to be okay with it for a while, but then it would eat at him a bit. He started wondering about Klemme's motive. I think the rabbi tried to keep in touch with him from time to time, to see if he was on the straight and narrow, and Matthew resented it. He said he didn't want any more help from 'that Jew.' He told me that just a week or so ago. Now are you going to tell me what this is about?"

"I appreciate your cooperation, Reverend," Mihdí said. "Jacob Klemme was murdered in his synagogue in Pine Bluff earlier this week. It appears that Skefton had the opportunity to commit the murder, so I was trying to establish whether he had a motive."

There was a silence on the other end for a few seconds.

"Well, I played right into that, didn't I?" the Rev. Elijah Crestwood finally said quietly. "What do you think now?"

"It certainly appears that Matthew could have a motive through his resentment of the help that Rabbi Klemme had given him," Mihdí expounded. "But I have also learned that he is trying to get his life in order and is trying to discover and accept guidance from the Bible and the church. At this stage all of it, pro and con, is just background. Neither I nor any judge would convict a person based on impressions. I have absolutely no evidence that Matthew had anything to do with this crime. I'll continue to give him the benefit of the doubt until such time as I do."

"I hope you do," Crestwood said. "He's a good kid. I can't imagine he would be involved in murder."

"That's an important endorsement, Rev. Crestwood," Mihdí said. "I believe that sometimes ministers know more about what goes on inside their parishioners' heads than they do. Thanks for your help."

"What was that about?" Andrea asked him when he returned to the living room where she was playing with the kids.

"Part of this case," Mihdí said. "I think I could have learned a lot from Rabbi Klemme. He sounds like he was quite an extraordinary guy."

"I thought that, too," said Andrea. "I only talked to him briefly at one VORP mediators' session, but he seemed to be really with it, both personally and professionally. I was hoping to invite him over for dinner sometime so we could get to know him better."

Mihdí found three flashlights, and he and the kids put on their coats so they could play outside for a few minutes while Andrea cleaned up the kitchen. When Mihdí and the children came back inside, both parents participated in getting them bathed and in bed, where Andrea read a story to Enoch while Mihdí read to Lua.

Once the kids were in bed, the couple sat together on the couch and relaxed over a cup of eggnog. They loved their moments alone together, which were far too few for either of their liking. Mihdí rubbed Andrea's feet and legs while they discussed the day. Andrea remembered Sam Schliebaum very well from a few events the older man had attended. She was also happy to hear that Mihdí had talked to Ray Engel, whom she hadn't seen for several years.

She was quite interested to hear about the connection between Jacob Klemme and Matthew Skefton through the Victim-Offender Reconciliation Program. Andrea was a member of the local VORP organization's board and was herself a trained mediator. She thought Skefton's name sounded familiar and that she had probably seen it in the quarterly reports received by the board, but she didn't know any details and had never met him herself.

Curiously, though, Andrea was most interested in hearing about Andy Sapp and what Darla Brownlee had said about the presence of racist groups in Pine Bluff. She was a psychologist and saw a number of clients in a private practice, but she and Lieutenant Brownlee had worked together on a couple of occasions to mediate between gang members and juvenile vandals and their victims. Darla Brownlee felt that the service that Andrea provided was one key to having fewer repeat offenders. The primary focus of the service was reconciliation, but this often involved restitution through work. In some cases, the offenders and the victims worked together to remove the stain of vandalism from the victim's property. This, in turn, created links between the two that helped break the cycle of victimization. Andrea expressed the opinion that a similar process could help in resolving issues of racism. She was extremely passionate about the idea of applying psychological and spiritual principles to social issues such as race relations, women's empowerment, and social justice and had worked with all sorts of groups and individuals on this type of work.

"Do you think there's any way to pry Andy Sapp away from this skinhead group?" she asked. "It sounds like he's got a good family background, but he's young enough to get in big trouble hanging out with those guys, especially since they're all older than he is."

"That's what I'm afraid of, too," Mihdí admitted. "I tried to slip in a suggestion about him getting together with Dooby and Evan at the community center. It looked like Andy might be interested, but if I push it, I feel like it could backfire."

"If you see him again, just make sure he's got it in his head," Andrea said. "You never know what could happen with your case. If that skinhead guy is involved with the murder, Andy may end up needing some new friends."

"I'm not sure whether to hope for that or not," Mihdí said with a sigh.

He and Andrea went up to bed, and she read while he worked a crossword puzzle for a while. Before turning out the lights, they shared a reading from the Bahá'í writings and had their ritual hug and kiss before saying goodnight.

Saturday, Day 4

The next day was Saturday, and Mihdí spent the day at home and with his family. Although the weather had been fairly warm through most of November, the forecast called for a snowstorm in the next few days, so Mihdí and Andrea worked together sealing off a few of their leakiest windows from the inside with shrinkwrap plastic. Mihdí also disconnected the hose, stowed it in the garage, and drained the gas from his lawn mower. Enoch and Lua helped their parents rake and pick up the last of the leaves on the lawn and patio.

Andrea had called their Bahá'í friends Premila and Vijaya Chandra from Naperville and arranged to meet them and their family at a park after lunch. The previous day's rain had disappeared, and it was a bit warmer, with bright sunshine. It was still jacket weather, but they took along extra sweatshirts in case it was colder in the openness of the park. They found, though, that Enoch and Lua, along with their friends Satish, Uma, and Mala Chandra, did so much running that they (and the parents keeping up with them) had to shed layers rather than add more.

At one point Mihdí, who had been sharing child-watching duties with Vijaya, passed near the bench where Andrea and Premila were sitting and chatting. Andrea hopped up and said, "Time for you to take a break, honey. Sit down and consult with Premila about your case." She walked toward where the kids were now playing.

Mihdí sat down on the bench and massaged his calves as he gave Premila an overview of the main facts of the case. Premila was currently staying home to care for Mala, the youngest of their three children, but she had a PhD in

Political Science, with a specialization in Criminal Justice. Before the birth of her oldest child, she had been a professor at a nearby university, and she continued to give guest lectures each semester.

When Mihdí had listed the people he considered the main suspects (without naming names), she immediately zeroed in on Brent Wiegand, "This guy sounds like he has nothing to lose. Just a few years out of high school, working at a dead-end job in a factory, involved with skinheads, bad attitude. . . ."

"Yeah, he doesn't have much going for him, I have to agree," said Mihdí. "And despite his account of his movements that day, I think he could have had time to get to the synagogue and kill the rabbi. What's your take on the Christian bookstore guy?"

"Well, of course, I can't say much, since I only have your very brief impressions to go on. But it seems that he is messed up, but maybe not so messed up as to commit murder."

"Even though his boss thinks he might be capable of it?"

"He probably is capable of it. But it sounds like this murder was unprovoked and from behind, right?"

Mihdí nodded.

"It would take someone with a lot of . . . something . . . to walk up behind a member of the clergy—of any religion—and whack him over the head. I'm not sure I can see a newly-minted Christian doing that, even to someone he's not fond of. Of course, there may be lots more under the surface, so he still bears investigation."

"And the real estate guy?"

"The way you described his alibi, I don't see how he could be involved. Might have hired a hitman or something, I suppose, but I don't think hitmen are easy to find. Most legitimate businessmen wouldn't have a clue how to go about that."

"Good points. And your take on the ex-fiancé?"

"We still have the problem of whacking someone on the head from behind, but at least he has a motive. Maybe it was personal for him; maybe he felt this rabbi was ruining his life. They could have had an argument, and he still could have been heated from that."

"Thanks for those thoughts, Professor," said Mihdí with a grin.

"I didn't really do anything other than echo back what you told me," she replied. "It sounds like you have your work cut out for you, though. Are you getting any pressure from the feds about hate crimes? I'd think they'd have their nose in on this."

"Apparently, they're watching the case, but haven't really gotten involved yet. My captain is fending them off for the present. But if I don't make some progress soon, they may step in."

"That might not be such a bad thing. They have resources most police departments can only dream about."

"That's true, but I'm not sure what good it would do them. I think this case will still come down to having lots of conversations with people until the right facts emerge. But if they take over the case, I've certainly got plenty of other things to do. I just hope justice is eventually served. It sounds like the rabbi was a really exceptional guy."

"I hate to change the subject, but did you ever succeed to your own satisfaction with homemade gulab jamun? I know you had tried several recipes and methods, but you weren't very happy with the first few."

From that point, talk turned to cooking, particularly of Indian food, which was a passion they both shared. When the parents felt that the kids had gotten a healthy dose of time in the park, the two families went to an Indian restaurant, where they were joined by Premila's parents, who were visiting from Texas. The Montgomerys returned home well after dark. Mihdí bathed the little ones, then Andrea got them into bed and read them stories.

After the kids were in bed, Andrea decided to take a hot bath to soak away the fatigue of the day. Mihdí got on the Internet and did some research on skinhead group activity in the Chicago suburbs. What he read confirmed the information that Darla Brownlee had given him. He thought it wouldn't hurt to interview Andy Sapp again to get more details about Brent Wiegand and the others in their little group. It appeared that the groups around the Chicago area were mostly just talk, but it certainly seemed that an impressionable young person might be inflamed to take action by the passionate rhetoric of the group. As often happened to him, Mihdí got totally absorbed in surfing from site to site on the Internet, and it was about 10:45 when he finally pried himself away and went to bed.

Mihdí felt as if he had just gotten to sleep when the telephone rang, but the clock showed that it was about 12:30 a.m. The call was from the police dispatcher, telling him that a man had been arrested in circumstances that might bear on the Klemme murder case and that he ought to come down to the station. Mihdí got dressed and drove there. As a police detective, such calls were inevitable, but as he grew older, it was more difficult to pry his eyes open and function at one hundred percent.

"What have we got?" he asked with a yawn when he checked in at the station.

The dispatcher pointed him to the lounge, "Officer Roggins brought the guy in."

Mihdí went to the lounge and found Tim Roggins drinking a cup of coffee and filling out the last parts of an arrest report. Roggins was built like a football player: very solid in the shoulders and torso, thin hips and massive muscular legs and arms. He had been a starter on the football team his last three years in college, but he had never really considered a career in the sport. Instead, he had studied criminal justice and had enrolled in the police academy as soon as he had graduated. Unlike Mihdí, Roggins was wide awake, and he hopped up to greet Mihdí when he saw him enter the lounge.

"Hey, Tim," Mihdí said, "how are you tonight?"

Roggins smiled. "Can't complain," he said, "although I usually do anyway. How's the wife and kids?"

"Asleep," Mihdí said, "which is where I should be, too. How are Janet and that new baby of yours?"

"Both doing fine," Roggins replied. "Jan would like me to get on days now that we have the baby. Guess I don't help out that much during the daytime, so she wants me to be there at night." Roggins had been on the force about four years. As with many new recruits, he had been assigned to the night shift, but he had enough seniority now that he could ask for a transfer to days.

"I can't say I ever enjoyed getting up in the middle of the night," Mihdí said, "but I have some great memories of walking around a dark house, putting a fussy baby back to sleep. I wouldn't trade those memories for anything."

"Thinking about it," said Roggins. "May win me over yet."

"So, who's this guy you brought in for me," Mihdí asked.

"Name is Sapp. Rick Sapp."

"What? That can't be. Andy Sapp, maybe, but not Rick."

"Don't know nothin' about that, but I arrested him in front of the syna-gogue with a can of spray paint. Just started to spray something on the wall when I stopped him. Caught him red-handed. Literally. Looked like he'd sprayed more on his hands than on the wall."

"How did you happen to arrive at just the right time?"

"Some lady called it in. She noticed a man dressed all in black, with a black ski mask pulled down over his face, walking through their neighbor-hood. Said the guy didn't really seem to be tryin' to hide. Just walking along the sidewalk, big as you please. But it looked suspicious to her."

"It's warm for November. There's certainly no need for a ski mask tonight."

"Guess that's what the caller thought, too. I was in the area and was first on the scene. Waited 'til Sapp started spraying the place so I could catch him in the act."

"Did Sapp resist arrest at all?"

"Nope. Just dropped everything and held out his hands for handcuffs. Been quiet ever since. He's in the interview room waiting for you."

"I wanted to ask you, Tim, have you been one of the officers taking extra passes down St. Andrews Drive?"

"Yep. I don't come on until 11:00, so I can't say I've seen much. I talked to one of the afternoon 'black and whites,' and he said none of them have seen anything worth reporting."

"Well, that's what I expected, but it's good to know."

Mihdí stood and pondered for a little while before going in to talk to Sapp. His earlier visit to Sapp's house had convinced him that neither Rick nor Andy would have murdered Rabbi Klemme. He figured that Sapp must be worried about Andy and was trying to protect him by diverting attention to himself. Mihdí opened the door and went in.

"Hi, Rick," he said.

"Oh, Montgomery, it's you." Sapp blushed a deep red.

"Yep, it's me," Mihdí said. He stood silent for a moment, looking at Sapp. "You know, Rick, I don't think Andy killed the rabbi. I doubt he had any-thing to do with it."

Rick looked at him with his jaw wide open. He started to stammer an objection, but Mihdí cut him off. "Tell me why you think he did."

Rick stared at him for a moment, then, as the realization dawned that Mihdí had figured out his motive, answered quietly, "I noticed that more patrol cars have been passing by our house lately. I figured you must have alerted them to Andy's activities so they could watch him."

Mihdí nodded. "I thought it was worth watching the situation a little more carefully," he said. "Was there more?"

Sapp looked defeated. "I searched Andy's closet while he was at school, and I found some spray-paint. I found a notebook where he had written a lot of racist crap, including a couple where he used the n-word. The newspaper had said it was hate language that had been painted on the synagogue wall. I figured Andy must have been surprised by the rabbi while he was doing it."

"Maybe," Montgomery said, "I'll need to talk to him about the previous graffiti incidents, but it doesn't feel to me like he is involved in this. I admire your sacrifice in trying to protect your son, Rick."

"Didn't work so well, huh?"

"No, it didn't work, but it has a certain nobility. Hey, the Beth Shalom congregation is planning to have a work day tomorrow . . . uh, today . . . to clean the graffiti off the walls. If you're willing to come and help, I'll see if we can make this whole thing go away. In the meantime, why don't you go home?"

Rick shook his hand warmly and wiped away tears as he left.

Mihdí realized how tired he was from a long day and from having his sleep interrupted. He drove home, went into the bedroom as quietly as possible, got back into his pajamas, slipped noiselessly into bed so as not to wake his wife, and fell back to sleep almost instantly.

Sunday, Day 5

Mihdí would have liked to sleep in on Sunday morning, particularly after his short night, but he wanted to help out the Beth Shalom congregation in cleaning up the synagogue. In fact, several members of the Bahá'í community had volunteered to help. Mihdí lumbered out of bed, put on some work clothes, and drove down to the synagogue, waking up a bit in the chill of the early morning.

When he got to the building, he saw that the previous night's spray paint had already been removed from the outside wall. He went inside and found quite a few people working and preparing to work. A number of the older members of the congregation were sitting in the pews, visiting and watching others work. Mihdí recognized one of them and greeted her, recalling her name in the nick of time.

"It's very nice to see you, Mrs. Fischbach," he said. "Have you quit for the day already?"

Ruth Fischbach laughed. "There are so many people here, they insisted that we sit down and let the younger folks work. I can't say I'm disappointed at that."

Ruth Fischbach was a bit over seventy, but she was only recently retired from a secretarial job at City Hall. She had lots of graying hair, pulled up into a bun at the back of her head. She wore blue jeans and a sweatshirt that hung over her small frame. She had survived breast cancer in her mid-sixties and had lost a lot of weight at that time, and she had managed to keep it off after her extensive radiation and chemotherapy treatments. Her hair had grown back to its full length, albeit with more gray in it. Now she was looking

71

recovered and healthy. Even in her work clothes, she held herself with a great deal of dignity. Her smile was genuine and seemed heartfelt.

Ruth introduced Mihdí to the woman she was sitting with, who turned out to be Miriam Fischbach, her husband's sister.

"Are all of these people members of the congregation?" Mihdí asked, after greeting Ruth's sister-in-law. "I didn't realize there were so many young people here now."

"Oh, no," she replied. "Not even a third are from Beth Shalom. Or do you say not even a third IS from Beth Shalom."

Mihdí laughed, "I was an English major in college, but I never know which of those is correct. Or which of those ARE correct. No, that one's definitely 'is.'"

It was Ruth Fischbach's turn to laugh. "We certainly appreciate all of the help," she said. "You know we are hosting this year's community Thanksgiving service on Wednesday evening, and we would hate to have the sanctuary in this horrible condition for that."

"Yes," said Mihdí, "I was thinking about that. I'm sorry the service will be at such a sad time for Congregation Beth Shalom."

"Rabbi Klemme was supposed to be the main speaker this time," Mrs. Fischbach said. "I guess they usually pick on the newest members of the Interfaith Alliance to speak at these things."

"I'm sure he would have added a wonderful presence to the event," Mihdí said. "Are you involved in the service yourself, Ruth?"

"Just the reception afterwards," she replied. "Hadassah is organizing that. We're veterans of this sort of thing, so we'll just arrive an hour or so before the service and get things set up and lay out some goodies."

"That will definitely be something to be thankful for," Mihdí observed with a grin.

Ruth Fischbach smiled.

Mihdí said, "I have to ask . . . Is Hadassah still all female, or has there been any change in that over recent years?"

"It's all female," Mrs. Fischbach confirmed. "Perhaps that change will come one day, but I am not aware of any such movement. Let me introduce you to some of the members of the congregation."

"That would be great," he said.

She led him around the sanctuary, introducing him to those who were free and pointing out some who were on ladders, or who were intent on their work. At one point, Mihdí found himself being introduced to Ahmad Muhammad, the owner of the coffee shop next door.

"Mr. Muhammad and I have met," Mihdí told Ruth Fischbach. "This is a wonderful thing you are doing here, Ahmad."

"The rabbi was a good friend," said Muhammad with a bow of respect to the dead, "and the congregation has been a good neighbor to me. It is the least I can do to repay their long kindness."

Mihdí discovered several other people from businesses on the block helping with the cleanup. His friend, Harry Katz, was holding a ladder as a younger man treated some paint on the wall with a special solvent. Rick and Carl Sapp had gotten there early and had been working together removing paint from the walls. Andy Sapp was not with them. Three members of the Bahá'í community were there: Isabelle Tourangeau, Cheryl Bryant, and Benjamin Avery. Mihdí was touched by the image of Jews, Christians, Muslims, Bahá'ís, and others working side by side to remove the defacement from the walls of the synagogue.

Mihdí also ran into Scott Craig, who apologized profusely for having missed their appointment. They made an appointment for late afternoon the next day at Craig's office.

After Mihdí had made the rounds, he found a job to do and started working up a sweat scrubbing and scraping. He ended up working next to Sandy Klarr, an employee of HisStory Christian Bookstore. The two of them chatted intermittently as they worked. Although they had not met previously, it turned out they knew a few people in common.

"I was in the store on Friday. I got a chance to talk to Stephanie Plante for a while when she was there."

"Yes, she told me that," Sandy said.

"I also met Matthew. Do you know if he's here somewhere?" he asked her.

Sandy replied immediately, "I would be very surprised if he was. I don't know him all that well, since we don't overlap all that much in the store. But it's my impression that it would take a direct visit from God Himself before

Matthew would miss church. I thought this act of service was more important for me, but I think his church is maybe more strict about attendance."

"What do you know about his church?" Mihdí asked.

"It's called Faith Tabernacle," she replied. "It's over in Bolingbrook or someplace like that."

"Is it affiliated with any denomination?"

"No, I think it's strictly congregational," Sandy answered. "I don't really know what the pastor teaches, but it all seems a bit too rigid to my mind."

"Any examples?"

"Well, I know Matthew never reads anything that isn't religious in nature and that he prefers just reading the Bible. Stephanie has had to talk to Matthew a few times to keep him from evangelizing with the customers too much and from talking them out of purchasing some of the books that he doesn't approve of. We mostly work at different times, so I haven't spent that much time with him myself; that's just what Stephanie has told me."

Mihdí devoted his attention to his scrubbing for a minute or two. After a good long pause he asked, "Does he have any problem with the synagogue being nearby?"

Sandy thought about that. "I've never heard him mention it, but like I said, I haven't worked with him that much."

"Do you know if Rabbi Klemme ever stopped into the store?" Mihdí asked.

"Oh, yeah. He stopped in a few times while I was working. He even bought a book now and then."

They both went back to their work for a little while. Out of the corner of his eye, Mihdí observed Sandy. She was quite short, with light brown hair and green eyes. Although she was white, her skin had the dark cast of a tan. She was dressed in a loose turquoise sweatsuit. She wore beat-up white tennis shoes with pink highlights and traces of housepaint on them. Work clothes.

Sandy broke the silence. "I just remembered that Matthew told me once that he hoped that the congregation here would sell the building. He wanted to see it turned into a Christian church. Personally, I really like having the synagogue in the neighborhood, although I suppose a church would also bring people into the store."

"Is HisStory open on Sundays?" Mihdí asked.

"No, it's not," Sandy replied. "Now that you mention it, the fact that some of our Jewish neighbors come over to the bookstore before or after their services is one thing that makes the synagogue a better source of customers than a church would be, since Christians would mostly only be here on Sundays when we're closed."

They both laughed at that.

"You know, in a way, Matthew was sort of biting the hand that fed him," Sandy said.

"In what way?"

"Well, Rabbi Klemme was the one who recommended him for the job."

"Really?" Mihdí asked in shock. "Stephanie Plante didn't say anything about that."

"Actually, she doesn't know about it," Sandy said. "I'm not sure I should have told you, but it seems like something you ought to know."

"Tell me about that, if you would," Mihdí encouraged.

"Jacob came over one day," she explained, "when I was alone in the store. He said that he had met a young man who would really benefit from working in a place like HisStory. He said the guy, who turned out to be Matthew, had gotten into some kind of trouble and that Jacob was trying to help him out. Jacob said he was meeting with Matthew later that day and was planning to casually mention our 'Help Wanted' sign to him. He hoped Matthew would come over that very day and fill out an application for the job. He specifically asked me if I could put in a good word for him to Stephanie without saying where the recommendation came from."

"And then it all happened just like that?" Mihdí asked.

"Uh-huh," acknowledged Sandy. "He came over that afternoon and filled out the application. I left it in Stephanie's box with a note saying that I had received a request from someone who did not want to be named and asking for her to give the applicant special consideration. Matthew was very eager in his interview, seemed to show good Christian values, and said he was willing to work hard, so Stephanie hired him."

"Did she ever ask you who had given you the recommendation?"

"Yes, she asked, but I told her I was sworn to secrecy, and she didn't press the matter."

"Do you think Matthew knew that the rabbi had put in a good word for him?"

"No, I don't think so. Matthew never mentioned it to me and hasn't ever said that to Stephanie, either. I'd say Jacob pulled it off pretty well. Until today, I was the only other one in on it."

Mihdí shook his head and said, "Matthew owes a great deal to that man. It's a shame he doesn't appreciate it more than he does."

After a short silence between them, Sandy asked, "You don't think Matthew is involved, do you?"

"I hope not," Mihdí answered. "A good churchgoing young man, steeped in study of the Bible . . . I hope he could never take a wrong turn like that. I like to think I am a reasonable judge of character, but it's part of my job to remain open even to possibilities that I don't like to contemplate."

Sandy nodded solemnly, and they both turned their attention back to their work.

By 1:00 p.m., there were more people idle than working. Mihdí came down from his ladder and stretched his arm muscles, which were a bit sore from the unaccustomed exertion. Before heading home, Mihdí headed to the restroom to clean up and found Scott Craig there washing his hands.

"I think it's pretty well licked," Mihdí said.

"Yes," said Craig curtly.

"I hear this is not the first incident of graffiti at the synagogue," Mihdí ventured.

"No, it isn't," Craig replied. "And it probably won't be the last, either."

"Are you thinking that this is just the way it is for Jews in America?" Mihdí asked him as they exited the restroom together.

"That's probably true," said Craig, "but just now I was thinking about this particular location. This part of town isn't what it was when the synagogue was built, or even a few years ago. The neighborhood has gone way downhill."

"I gather you support a move to a different part of town," Mihdí said.

"Absolutely!" answered Craig vehemently. "There are better, more friendly and more convenient locations than this by far. It's overdue for us to find one. Maybe Rabbi Klemme would still be alive if we had moved last year."

"Oh," said Mihdí, a bit startled. "Do you think the murderer was from this neighborhood?"

"That certainly wouldn't surprise me," Craig said, "but I was really just thinking that things would be that much different if we had moved. The old folks seems to think that we'll be able to revitalize the congregation down here, but that's just stupid. The only way to fix our problems is to move on."

"Tell me more about that," asked Mihdí.

"There are so many problems with this congregation, it just makes me crazy," said Craig. "But the biggest one is that the members are so old. Schliebaum's nearly ninety, and he isn't even the oldest active member. I don't think we have more than five families under forty, and it's not getting better. Klemme brought in a few new younger folks, but they'll all leave now; they only attended because of him, they don't care about the temple itself. And now the only way to get a good rabbi this time will be to move. Who will want to come to this place and face the possibility of being killed?"

"You feel that the congregation's choice not to move is pretty much directly responsible for the rabbi's death, then?" Mihdí inquired.

"It's hard to think otherwise," Craig said. "If people would just wake up and realize that people today don't want to live in the past, we might be able to have a decent synagogue. I always feel like I have to shake things up a bit, since these old fogies just want things to stay the same forever and ever, amen."

By this time, Craig had his jacket on. He told Mihdí he would see him the next day and left.

* * *

That evening was the Bahá'í Nineteen-Day Feast, a gathering held on the first day of each Bahá'í month. It is one of the primary events in the Bahá'í calendar, and Andrea and Mihdí made an effort to get their children to it as often as possible. Enoch and Lua didn't mind, as they had some good Bahá'í friends they enjoyed seeing.

Mihdí helped get the kids into their shoes and coats while Andrea gathered up a few letters and other correspondence to share at the Feast. As the Local Spiritual Assembly secretary, she had a responsibility to make sure such things were presented at the Feast. When they were all ready, they got into

Andrea's car, a ten-year-old dark green Toyota Camry, and drove to the home of Behzad and Fereshteh Rouhani, the hosts for this Feast. Before they went in, Mihdí reminded the kids that they needed to enter the house respectfully and take their seats quietly to maintain a prayerful atmosphere.

Behzad and Fereshteh's house was immaculately kept. Other people had arrived before Mihdí and his family, but Mihdí could still see that every chair, pillow, throw, picture, and rug was exactly in its place. Bezhad was seventy-eight and was a retired radiologist. In his retirement years, he had decided to get a degree in religious studies and had gotten his Master's degree the previous year from the University of Chicago. Fereshteh was seventy and still extremely active in the community. She represented the Bahá'ís in the Interfaith Alliance. Fereshteh had not worked outside the home but had somehow created a large network of friends and colleagues all around the region. She and Behzad had immigrated to the United States from Iran in the 1950s and had raised their family in this house in Pine Bluff. Now that their children were parents and grandparents themselves and were scattered throughout the world, the couple devoted their considerable energy to the activities of the Pine Bluff Bahá'í community.

The Feast, like all Bahá'í Feasts, had three separate parts: the devotional, the consultative, and the social portions. The hosts had chosen a number of short readings and prayers for the devotional portion. Fereshteh took Mihdí aside just before the devotions and asked if he would chant a prayer to open the devotions and then lead everyone in a few songs at the end. Since his promotion to detective, Mihdí no longer had time to sing in a choir, but he had a rich bass voice and was happy to get a chance to sing now and then at Bahá'í events.

When the devotions had ended, all of the children went to the basement for children's classes with Cheryl Bryant and her teenage daughter, Corinne, while the adults consulted on the affairs of the community. Fereshteh, as the chair of the Assembly, guided the meeting, but Andrea was the one to share most of the information. The coming termination of the lease for the Bahá'í Center was a topic of great interest, but much of the time was spent on consulting how to launch an upcoming project for two neighborhood children's classes in the new year.

As the consultation wound down, Behzad laid out some refreshments. The children came up from the basement and joined the adults for cookies, tea and juice, plus some fresh baklava that Fereshteh had made. A bit before 9:00, the Montgomerys managed to pry Lua and Enoch away from their friends and leave. While they had been inside at the Rouhanis, it had started to snow, but the snow had not yet begun to stick to the roads. The silently falling snow seemed to spread its influence over them, and there was no conversation as they drove home. They all went to bed quickly once they arrived.

Monday, Day 6

On Monday morning, Mihdí hurried to get his snow blower out to clear the sidewalks and the driveway of the four inches of snow that had fallen overnight. It was still snowing lightly, but he hoped that there wouldn't be much more accumulation. Both cars were in the garage, so he didn't need to clean them off.

Mihdí had scheduled a meeting of all the police personnel involved in any way in the Klemme case. It was a habit of his to ask others to join him to consider the facts of a case, and he found that a good, open consultation would usually open new directions and produce more creative thinking than he could do on his own. Originally, Captain Sterling and the other brass weren't very excited about the idea. They thought it would be a distraction and a waste of time for officers only peripherally involved in a case to spend time talking about it. But after more than three years of Mihdí demonstrating results from the consultations, nobody was inclined to fight them anymore.

The meeting had been scheduled for 8:30, but the snow had delayed Darla Brownlee and Beth Carr, so they weren't able to begin until just before 9:00. Mihdí had invited Darla, Beth, and Kurt Childs. He had also invited Tim Roggins, but Tim was off Sunday and Monday, so he wasn't able to come in. Mihdí had asked the patrol captain if one of the other beat cops that had been patrolling the neighborhood around the Sapp house could come, but none of them had shown up. Montgomery had extended a courtesy invitation to Captain Sterling, but he didn't expect him, either.

Mihdí began, "Let me just remind you of our purpose, since it's been a while since some of you have been in on one of these consultations. We're here to try to find the truth. It's not important whose mouth it comes out of, it's only important that we find whatever truth we can. Once a thought is 'on the table,' it belongs to the group, so you don't have to feel like you have to defend your own idea just because it's yours. Feel free to build on previously stated ideas. We always hope that the spark of differing ideas will shed some light on the facts of the case. We'll only go for as long as it seems that things are progressing. Does that work for all of you?"

Everyone nodded their agreement to the purpose as Mihdí had stated it.

"Let me tell you what I know. Rabbi Klemme was discovered in the sanctuary, with a candelabra lying near him."

"Wait, sorry," said Beth Carr. "What's a can-dull-a-ber?"

"Candelabra," Mihdí corrected. "It's a candlestick holder with places for multiple candles. I looked it up earlier, because I wasn't sure whether one would say 'candelabra' or 'candelabrum.' It turns out you can say either, but 'candelabra' is more common these days."

"Right," Beth said skeptically, "very common, I'm sure."

Mihdí continued, "The rabbi's blood was on the candelabra, and the coroner has confirmed that the cause of death was trauma to the head, almost certainly caused by the candleholder. There were anti-Semitic slogans and swastikas spray-painted on the walls. This was not the first instance of defacement of the synagogue in recent years. On three other occasions, slogans were spray-painted on the front of the building, and once there were some swastikas. I suspect most of you were aware of those when they happened. Nobody has yet been arrested for those crimes. That's the part I think you all knew already."

"Everything points to an obvious conclusion," interjected Kurt Childs.

"I agree," Mihdí said, "all of these facts point to a case of interrupted vandalism turned to murder. There are a couple of others things, though, that make me wonder a bit about it. First, I called the murder weapon a candelabra, which it is, of course. But more precisely, it was a hanukkia, often known as a menorah. You may be familiar with them as a symbol of Hanukkah. It is not normal for one to be out this long before Hanukkah begins. According to Sam Schliebaum, president of Beth Shalom synagogue, this one was kept in the supply room off the sanctuary, just to the right of the front door. This makes the interrupted vandalism explanation a bit awkward, as the vandal would have had to go to the storage room, grab the hanukkia, then strike the rabbi. There are other ways it could have gone down, of course, but it makes things a bit more complex.

"Another thing that seemed a bit odd to me was the slogans themselves. There were two swastikas, and there were three phrases: 'Death to Jews,' 'Christ-killers,' and 'Liberate Palestine.' To my mind, that last one doesn't fit with the others. If we were talking about some kind of anti-Semitic group or individual, you might see the swastikas and the first two phrases, but I can hardly imagine them writing that last one. And if we were talking about a radical Palestinian Arab activist, it's hard to picture them worrying about Jews being 'Christ-killers' or using a swastika, for that matter."

"It's pretty difficult to imagine that there was a racist and an Arab terrorist working together on this," said Darla Brownlee with a slight smile.

Mihdí chuckled. "Indeed. That would be even more unusual than a single individual writing all of those things."

Beth Carr piped up at this moment. "I got a fax this morning from the crime lab. They said that the hairs that were found on the wall of the synagogue definitely belonged to the vic. But they said that the stuff on the hairs included both blood and paint. Having collected those hairs myself, I can tell you that means that at least some of the painting happened after the rabbi was killed. I called the technician down there and he confirmed that there was also evidence of backspray on the rabbi's clothes, indicating that the perp must have been practically standing over the body while doing some of the painting."

Lieutenant Brownlee offered, "It's hard to imagine a gang member being surprised in the act of vandalism going to a supply closet to grab a menorah, killing the rabbi by whacking him over the head with it, then standing over his dead, bloody body to complete a slogan."

They all muttered their agreement with that assessment.

"I think there are actually a number of ways this crime could have gone down," Mihdí said. "I want to work through at least a couple of them so we have a better idea of what we're talking about. If you think I'm missing something or have some other ideas, jump in at any time.

"Here's one that I think is reasonable. Someone, let's say it's a male, came into the synagogue with the idea of doing graffiti. That seems likely, since he must have brought spray-paint and must have been wearing gloves. Some of the graffiti is so high, he must have moved a chair or stool from somewhere to stand on. So, he came in and started doing the graffiti. Apparently, Rabbi Klemme usually left the front door unlocked when he was there so people could come into the sanctuary and pray or pass through to the office area. So, while the vandal was spray-painting, he heard someone coming. He hid in the storage cabinet near the front door. He saw it was the rabbi and decided to kill him. So, he grabbed the hanukkia, sneaked up on the rabbi as he was looking at the unfinished graffiti, and whacked him. Then he proceeded to finish the graffiti."

Beth Carr looked skeptical. "I don't get why a vandal would decide to switch from graffiti to murder just because the rabbi caught him. How about something more like this? The perp came in with the intention of murder, which he intended to cover up to look like interrupted vandalism. He knew the rabbi and enticed him into the sanctuary, where he killed him, then did all the graffiti after that."

"That makes more sense to me in some ways," Kurt Childs replied. "If the rabbi was in the building, it would be tough for someone to get too far along with the vandalism without making enough noise to be discovered, or at least taking that risk. If the rabbi wasn't there, wouldn't he have had to come right into the sanctuary himself to discover the vandal?"

"There's a back door, closer to the office area," Mihdí said. "A parking spot in the back was reserved for Rabbi Klemme, but even when he walked to the synagogue, he usually entered through the back."

Kurt nodded. "Well, if Rabbi Klemme normally came in through the back and left the front door unlocked, your first way seems reasonable. The murderer could have come in through the front and started on the graffiti, regardless of whether he planned the murder. Then later, when he heard someone coming, he hid."

Mihdí considered. "It's possible," he said. "The door from the sanctuary that leads into the administrative area is usually closed. That door opens into a hallway, which leads past restrooms, around a corner, and past some classrooms before you get to the office, just by the back door. Unless the vandal was pretty loud, it seems quite possible Klemme wouldn't have heard him from the office. Although there might have been some noise from moving a chair or table or ladder or whatever . . ."

They all sat and thought for a little while.

Darla Brownlee broke the silence. "From what you said earlier, the murder was the first thing, then the graffiti came afterward, right? The body was not far from the door to the office area, right? Perhaps the rabbi was expecting someone and met him at the front door, and the perp killed him as they made their way towards the office. Did you check Klemme's calendar for that day?"

"He didn't have any appointments before 6:00 p.m., and the murder happened most likely between 1:00 p.m. and 4:00 p.m.," said Mihdí, "but I think there's a problem with your idea. The murder weapon, the hanukkia, came from the synagogue's storage area. I suppose it's possible that the rabbi and the murderer stopped at the closet and got it for some reason, or that the murderer had gotten it earlier and brought it with him. But it seems more likely that it was a matter of opportunity. The murder either wasn't planned and the hanukkia was the closest weapon at hand, or the murderer planned to hide in the closet all along and knew there would be a weapon there. Also, the body wasn't found along the normal route people would take from the front door to the office. The front door opens into a small entrance area from which you enter the back of the sanctuary. You would then normally turn right and walk along the back of the pews to the wall, then turn left and follow that wall forward to the door that opens into the administrative area. The rabbi's body was found along that same wall, but closer to the front of the sanctuary, so it's not likely he was on the way between the front door and the office. It would have been a bit dark at 6:00 p.m., so it's perfectly reasonable for Scott Craig not to have noticed the body when he came through the sanctuary and found the graffiti on his way to the office. As it was, he said he didn't discover Klemme until he returned, after finding the office empty."

Beth Carr spoke up again, "How about if there were two people? One came prepared to vandalize the place. He painted a few slogans and left, before the rabbi arrived. The other one came and found the graffiti and the rabbi. Maybe he made some excuse to go to the closet, grabbed that Hanukkah thing or whatever it's called, and killed the rabbi. Then he did some more graffiti so it would look like he was caught in the act."

Everyone nodded in appreciation about how well that idea worked.

Mihdí said, "Would that mean that the vandal left some spray-paint in the sanctuary that the murderer found later? The other possibility would be that the murderer killed Klemme, then went out and bought some spray-paint, came back and finished the slogans. If I were the murderer, that would seem too risky to me."

After a moment, Beth Car responded. "It definitely has a problem, yes. The vandal would have no reason to leave perfectly good spray-paint there. A careless one might leave empties, but why leave enough for a whole 'nother slogan? It's just wasteful. They could vandalize something else entirely with all that extra paint, or they could have done their own additional graffiti before leaving. It's not impossible, but it's kooky."

"The other way around seems even less likely," replied Kurt Childs. "Someone came and murdered the rabbi and left his body in the sanctuary, then a vandal came along and calmly painted graffiti around, stepping over the dead body in the process."

"Hmm, yeah," confirmed Mihdí. "Very unlikely. So, I think that makes the two-criminal version implausible. I'd say we're back to a murderer who wanted to make it look like vandalism or a vandal who decided to take the opportunity to do murder. Anyone disagree with that assessment?"

"Not me," Lieutenant Brownlee said. "I don't think we should rule out a two-criminal scenario, because we've all seen stranger things than that, but it seems more likely to be a single individual. If it is, what's the motive?"

"Yeah," replied Mihdí, "that's the next question, I think. I haven't been able to make sense of the graffiti itself." He reminded them of the odd combination of slogans that had been found. "Maybe all three of them could feel like hate speech to a Jew, but it doesn't seem likely that an Arab political activist would write the slogan about 'Christ-Killers,' and an American anti-Semite probably wouldn't like Palestinians much better than Jews. So I'm not even sure who could have written all three of them."

"What about a Jew?" asked Darla Brownlee. "Perhaps a Jew who was trying to cover up a murder would feel them all as attacks and wouldn't realize how incongruous they would all be as a whole."

"Interesting thought," replied Beth. "I was thinking that it could be someone smarter or dumber than we're considering."

"Smarter or dumber?" Kurt asked. "What on earth do you mean by that?"

"Well," she replied. "If it was someone smarter, maybe they thought that writing slogans that don't fit together would make matching a specific profile of the killer more difficult for us. Maybe they were thinking we would guess that the motive couldn't be anti-Semitism because of the Palestinian slogan. Then they would have still said what they wanted to say, but they would have scattered the suspicion. See what I mean?"

"That's good thinking," Mihdí said. "But how about someone dumber? What did you mean by that?"

"Well," she said, "to you it's obvious that these three don't fit together. But if you were just some dumb vandal trying to terrorize Jews, you might just get on the Internet and find some slogans that people had used and use a few of them without really knowing all the implications of each."

They all laughed. "We certainly can get too clever for ourselves sometimes, can't we?" Mihdí said with a laugh. "When you read people's arguments on the Internet, it is very clear that lots of them are only repeating garbage they've heard elsewhere and really don't completely understand. You could be right about this."

"We didn't really get to motives yet, did we?" Darla asked. "I think we got sidetracked a bit on the meaning of the graffiti itself. What could motivate someone to do this crime?"

"Let me start by sharing something I found on the Internet," Mihdí said. "It's from a book in 1995 by Ruth Rendell called *The Reason Why*. In it, Rendell came up with six basic motives, based on depictions of fictional killers in literature, as to why people commit murders: gain, revenge, escape, altruism or duty, insanity, and impulse or curiosity." Mihdí wrote those six together at the top of the room's white board. "There are many ways these can each play out, but they might give us some ideas to apply to this case. Let's brainstorm possibilities. Here, I'll write them on the whiteboard. Just call 'em out, and we'll evaluate each one later."

"Anti-Semitism," said Beth.

"A grudge against the rabbi," offered Kurt.

"Trying to drive the congregation out," Mihdí wrote as he said it. "I hadn't gotten a chance to tell you about this yet. The congregation voted a year ago to stay where they are, but there are some in the congregation who would like to see them move to a new location that's not so close to downtown. What else do you think of?"

"Love triangle," Darla said. When everyone laughed, she added, "Hey, it's a common motive—if there's a cover-up involved, we don't know what the murder is really about."

"It's a valid point," said Mihdí. "We have to keep in mind when we're brainstorming that we're not supposed to evaluate yet. And actually, the rabbi was dating a woman who broke up with her previous boyfriend, so the idea is not at all far-fetched."

"Money," Beth added.

"That's good," replied Kurt. "Or some combination of motives, like a grudge over money or driving the congregation out because of a love triangle. Well, maybe not that combo."

"A combination," Mihdí said. "That's quite likely. Thanks, Kurt. What else?"

"Internecine struggle," Darla volunteered.

"What the heck is that?" Kurt asked. "I don't think I've ever heard that word."

"It means some kind of struggle within a group," Darla said.

"So in this case that would mean within Congregation Beth Shalom, I suppose," Kurt answered.

"Yep, that's what I had in mind."

They sat for a while in silence, but nobody really had a lot more to offer.

"A personal grudge is a pretty big topic and could have lots of subareas," Mihdí said. "It seems like I need to learn more about the victim's personal life in order to explore that one."

"The same thing is true about money," Beth said. "There are lots and lots of ways that could lead to murder."

"Good point," Mihdí replied. "I'll need to look into that more carefully as well."

"What do we have in the way of suspects?" Darla asked.

"Nothing solid at all," Mihdí said. "I do have some people who seem to have some connection, but I haven't had much chance to follow up yet. Let me give you the run down on what I have to date.

Mihdí told them what he knew about Andy Sapp and the incident with Rick Sapp being arrested.

"I've talked to Darla about it, and she had one rather thin lead on skinhead activity in town. I verified that the name in her file is the same guy that Andy Sapp has been hanging around with. I talked to the guy the other day, and he has an attitude as big as all outdoors, but he claims he was at work until 3:00 p.m., then took the bus home. If all that is true, I don't think he could have had time to commit the murder. Kurt, I think I sent you an e-mail asking you to check on his timecard."

"Yep," said Kurt. "I've got it on my list to do that today."

Mihdí continued with his rundown. "Next door to the synagogue is a coffee shop run by an Arab Muslim from Tunisia. I don't think he's involved in any way."

"Even though he's Muslim?" Beth asked.

"Yes," said Mihdí. "There is absolutely nothing that I've found that suggests any anti-Semitism or violence in his character or beliefs. He seems to be mostly an entrepreneur, trying to make it in a tough business."

"If you say so," Beth replied.

"Also on the block is a Christian bookstore. One of the employees is a born-again and somewhat fanatical Christian who has some personal history with the rabbi and seems to dislike him. I got some new information on him but haven't completed all of the necessary investigation."

Mihdí also told them about Charlie Richardson and his connection to the possible move of the synagogue. He mentioned that the corner deli would probably move if the synagogue moved and that Neil Hoffman hoped Richardson would be interested in that.

"But Richardson has a solid alibi," added Mihdí. "I talked to a couple that he directed me to and they confirmed that he spent the entire afternoon of the murder with them, from 1:00 to 6:00 p.m., showing them houses in Pine Bluff.

Finally, Mihdí filled them in on what he knew about Scott Craig, including the fact that Craig had stood him up on Friday, but that they had an appointment for that afternoon.

"Well, where does that leave us?" Mihdí asked.

Darla thought Brent Wiegand was the most likely suspect based on his avowed racism and the tie-in to the graffiti. Kurt was more inclined toward thinking that Charlie Richardson must have some connection because of his potential financial gain from the congregation moving. Beth felt that Mihdí should dig deeper into Ahmad Muhammad, thinking that it was too much of a coincidence for an Arab Muslim to be right next door to the murder of a rabbi and not be involved. Mihdí was leaning towards Matthew Skefton as his prime suspect because he thought he would be most fanatical early on in his religious indoctrination. They all agreed that Scott Craig needed to be investigated further as well.

After that, the four of them consulted for about ten more minutes, reviewing the facts and trying to figure out what they could deduce. They quickly decided that they did not have enough facts to make any further conclusions.

Mihdí summarized, "We agree that it is most likely that a single person committed all of the crime in this case, although there are anomalies. There must have been some premeditation to this crime, at least on the day of the murder, because the scenario of the rabbi surprising someone writing graffiti on the wall doesn't fit all the facts. If the vandalism is only there to cover up the murder, the true motive could be just about anything. The possible skinhead connection seemed to fit best with the idea of vandalism, not premeditated murder, as we have no evidence of any past violence related to Wiegand or other racist groups. We're pretty divided about which of the suspects stands out, but they all need to be investigated more. I need to push a little harder on some of the alibis to see if they hold up. Perhaps the biggest need is to find out more about the victim to see what kind of motive fits best with his life and death. Does that cover it?"

"Sounds right to me," said Kurt Childs, and the others nodded their assent.

As they were wrapping up, Darla Brownlee's assistant came in and passed a phone message to her.

"Here's a coincidence," Darla said after reading the message. "I just got a call from a Captain Bertram in Bridgeview," she replied, "Brent Wiegand was arrested early this morning for vandalism at some kind of Islamic Community Center. He had broken in and had messed things up a bit, throwing books around, knocking stuff over and painting slogans on the wall. Sounds similar enough to what happened at the synagogue that I thought you might be interested."

"I'm definitely interested," Mihdí asked. "Where is he now?"

"He's at the lockup at Bridgeview right now," she told him. "Bertram asked me if I wanted to interview him, and I said I did. So, I'm heading up there right now. Wanna come?"

"I've already got my coat on," Mihdí said, following her out to the parking lot.

The drive over took them a bit less than twenty minutes. When they arrived, they went through a standard security screening, then waited in a holding area while Wiegand was brought from his cell to an interview room. Once he was inside, the two Pine Bluff detectives entered the room and sat down across the table from Brent Wiegand. They had agreed that Brownlee would initiate the questioning.

"You are Brent Wiegand?" she asked the prisoner.

"That's right," Wiegand answered, "as I'm sure you know, since I just talk-ed to your pig buddy here a few days ago." Wiegand was still in a preliminary lockup, waiting to be processed, so he was still wearing his own clothes, not an orange jumpsuit. He had on sneakers, jeans, a dark t-shirt, and a hooded sweatshirt pulled over it. They had learned from his arrest sheet that he was twenty-two years old. He had blue eyes and brown hair, and his beard and moustache were very thin and spotty, as if the right hormones hadn't quite kicked in to grow anything fuller.

Brownlee continued, "I am Lieutenant Darla Brownlee of the Pine Bluff Police Department, and, as you know, this is my colleague, Detective Mihdí Montgomery."

91

Wiegand didn't respond.

"I understand that you were caught in the act of vandalizing an Islamic Community Center earlier today, is that correct?" she asked.

"That's what I'm accused of," Wiegand said. "I don't think I need to answer your questions without having a lawyer present."

"That's correct, Mr. Wiegand," Brownlee replied, "as I'm sure you were told when you were brought in here. Actually, we're not involved in that case, and it is of no interest to us. We're more interested in activities of a similar nature in Pine Bluff. Do you know anything about that?"

Wiegand shrugged. "Midi-boy already asked me about that. Like I told 'em, I don't know nuthin' about it."

"What do you think about Jews, Mr. Wiegand?" Mihdí asked him.

"I don't give a rip about Jews, Islams, or whatever," Wiegand replied. "I just want to be able to live in America like my ancestors done. Anybody else can just go back where they came from and leave this country to white guys like me."

"You told me earlier that you didn't know anything about the incident last week, which also involved spray paint and graffiti, at the Congregation Beth Shalom Synagogue," Mihdí said. "Are you still sticking with your story? It sounds like that would be right up your alley . . ."

"If you're trying to pin that murder on me," Wiegand said. "I ain't sayin' another word without a lawyer."

"We can't force you to talk, of course, as you know," Mihdí said. "Can anyone verify your whereabouts that day?"

"I worked until 3:00 p.m.," he said, "then I get home around 3:45, and some guys usually drop in about then."

"What guys, exactly?" asked Detective Brownlee.

"I don't know who was there a week ago, for God's sake."

"You said you usually get home at 3:45," Mihdí said. "Are you certain that you did that last Tuesday?"

"Yeah, as a matter of fact," Wiegand said. "I take the bus every day, and it lets me off at the end of my block at the same time within a minute practically every day."

"You don't own a car?" Brownlee asked.

92

"Nope," Wiegand replied. "Can't afford one."

"Could anyone confirm that you were on the bus that day?" Brownlee inquired.

"Doubt it," Wiegand said, hotly. "Like I told your sidekick here the other day, I don't know any of 'em, and it was just a day like any other."

Mihdí asked, "Did Andy Sapp drop by that evening?"

"Like I said, I don't know," Wiegand snapped. "He's there a lot, but not every night, so I just don't know."

"Did you ever talk to Andy about coming to the Islamic Center last night?" Mihdí asked.

"No. He's too young to understand all the stuff I do, so I left him out of it."

"So you've never discussed participating in any illegal activity with him?"

"I'm not answering that question," Wiegand replied. "Seems like you're trying to trap me."

Mihdí chuckled. "Well, I can see why you would think so, but I'm really not. I'm concerned about Andy Sapp and I wanted to know if you've been involving him in anything that I would need to be worried about. You've certainly given him some of your flyers."

"He saw the flyers himself and asked about them. He's smart enough to see what's happening to decent white people in this country."

"I guess I'm not that smart," said Mihdí, "because I'm not seeing it."

"Well, you wouldn't, would you," Wiegand said, defiantly.

"I think we're done here," interjected Detective Brownlee.

"I guess we are," said Mihdí, "for now." He turned to Brent Wiegand. "Since nobody can verify your alibi for the synagogue crimes, we may be in and out of your life for a while. Based on the circumstances of your arrest, it doesn't seem like you'll be going anywhere for a while."

Wiegand snorted and turned away.

The two detectives left the interview room and informed the attending officer that they were done. They asked the duty officer if they could talk to whoever was handling the case and sat down to wait in the holding area.

Brownlee observed, "He didn't really give us anything at all to implicate him in the Klemme case."

"No," Mihdí agreed. "He certainly didn't clear himself, but neither did we get anything useful. Truth be told, he doesn't seem smart enough to plan and carry out premeditated murder and get away with it. He got caught this time in the middle of the night, for heaven's sake. How could he have murdered Klemme in the middle of the day and not made a mess of it? And if we verify his work schedule, he wouldn't have had a big window in which to get to the synagogue and murder Klemme before 4:00."

"It's an hour," Darla said. "That's plenty of time."

"Yeah, I guess you're right," Mihdí admitted. "Perhaps the bus driver or one of the regular riders will be able to confirm or deny his story. Anyway, I'll follow up on the parts we can confirm and see if that clarifies anything. If we catch him in a lie, that would tell us something."

A few moments later, a young woman came out of the office area and approached them.

"Hi," she said. "I'm Detective Owens. I'm handling the incident at the Islam Center."

Darla and Mihdí stood and offered their hands.

"I'm Lieutenant Brownlee, and this is Detective Montgomery from Pine Bluff. We have some interest in your perp regarding another crime, and we just got done talking to him."

"Right," said Detective Owens. "Come on back to my desk. What can I do for you?"

"We were just wondering if there was anything you could add to what we heard from him," Darla replied.

"Did you already see the arrest report?" Owens asked.

Darla nodded.

"I can't add much to that, I guess. We got an anonymous tip that there was something going on at the Islam Center, so we sent a car over to check it out."

"Do you know where the tip came from?" Mihdí asked.

"Not yet, but I'll send you an e-mail once we find that out. Anyway, they caught this Wiegand guy spray-painting slogans in the main hall there. He hadn't actually gotten that far along, and he was caught in the act."

"Was he wearing gloves, by any chance?" Mihdí asked.

"Yeah, he was. They're right here, actually." She handed Mihdí the evidence bag that contained the gloves.

"I see both black and red paint on these," Mihdí observed. "Had he used both colors on the walls?"

"Nope. Just the black. He must have done this before."

"Just what I was thinking," Mihdí said.

Darla and Mihdí looked at each other to confirm that neither of them had anything else to ask. Darla said, "Unless you have something else for us, we don't need to keep you. Thanks for your time."

They chatted about their families as they drove back to the Pine Bluff Police Station. When he got back to his office, Mihdí checked in with Kurt Childs about Brent Wiegand.

"I talked to Wiegand's supervisor," Kurt said. "He confirmed that Wiegand was at work last Tuesday and that he had clocked out at 3:01 p.m. He didn't know if Wiegand had gotten on the bus, but he asked around quickly to see if anyone remembered. One of Wiegand's coworkers, who rides the same bus, confirmed that Wiegand usually rides the bus, but couldn't remember for sure if he did last Tuesday."

"That's great stuff, Kurt," said Mihdí. "Thanks!"

"Ah, but there's more," Kurt said. "I ran Wiegand's name and found him in our databases. He hasn't been convicted of anything or even arrested, as far as I can find. But he was a suspect in a murder investigation in New Lenox just this last May. Wiegand was seen in the area the night that a . . . let's see . . . Silas Pattison was stabbed to death. But there were no witnesses and no murder weapon, so New Lenox couldn't establish if Wiegand was involved. He denied it, of course."

"That's quite interesting," Mihdí said. "Could you ask New Lenox to send the file to me, in case there's anything else in it?"

"Will do!"

"Could you also see if we can get a warrant to search Wiegand's place? Clear it with Bridgeview PD as well because we don't want to tread on their investigation."

"Yes, sir. I'll text you when we've got it."

"Thanks, Kurt."

Mihdí walked over to Darla's office and told her what he had learned.

She said, "The fact that he was at work on Tuesday doesn't really tell us any more than we already knew, other than confirming it. If he rode the bus, he probably couldn't have committed the murder, but since we don't have any verification about the bus, we can't say one way or the other. And the connection to the other murder doesn't give us anything, either, does it? There doesn't seem to be any connection to your case."

Mihdí decided he wanted to talk to Andy Sapp. As a close friend of Wiegand's, the boy couldn't be trusted as a reliable witness, but the detective wanted to tell Sapp directly about Wiegand's arrest for two reasons. He wanted to see Sapp's reaction, which he thought might tell him more about whether there had been any discussion about the vandalism at the Islamic Center or about other such activities. Mihdí also hoped that if he showed this much interest in the boy, Andy might feel more inclined to spend at least some of his time with a better set of friends, perhaps the musicians that Mihdí had mentioned to him.

He drove over to the school and once again had Andy Sapp paged to the office. The whole interview took only a few minutes. Andy seemed honestly surprised about Wiegand's arrest and the reason for it. Mihdí asked him if he had seen spray paint or other suspicious items around Wiegand's apartment.

Andy thought about it for a moment before saying, "I've never seen anything like that in his apartment, but I did once see Brent unlock a closet down the hall from his place. When I asked him about it, he said it was included in his rent because his apartment didn't have much storage space in it. And we've talked about tagging with spray paint."

"Oh, that's helpful," Mihdí said. "Have you had a chance to check out that community center I mentioned the other day?"

"Not really," Andy said. "I did walk by it the other day, just to see where it was. I might go there sometime."

Mihdí smiled at the fact that Andy had remembered his comment and followed up. After that, neither of them had any more to say to each other, so Mihdí didn't prolong the visit.

* * *

Mihdí had received a text from Kurt Childs saying that a warrant had been secured to search Brent Wiegand's apartment, and since Mihdí was already nearby, he took the opportunity to stop by. The apartment was located in a rundown, two-story house on a rundown block in a rundown neighborhood. Mihdí knocked on the front door of the house. An elderly woman answered the door.

"Are you the owner of this house, by any chance?" Mihdí asked.

"Yes, my husband and I own this house," she replied.

Mihdí introduced himself and showed her his badge. "I have a warrant to search Mr. Wiegand's apartment. Could you open the door for me, please?"

"I don't get around as easily as I used to, Detective," she said. "But let me get you my key and you can help yourself."

"Thank you very kindly, ma'am," Mihdí said, as she was turning away to get the key. "I understand there's a closet in the hallway that goes along with that apartment. I'd like to see that as well."

She said, "The same key opens the closet. I won't be a moment." She was back in less than a minute with the key.

"I'll bring it back when I'm done, ma'am," Mihdí said.

He went around to the side door, which was unlocked, then up the stairs to the second floor. Since Mihdí had been there before, he knew the layout. There were two apartments upstairs. Wiegand's door was just at the top of the stairs, and the other apartment was at the end of the hall. Mihdí could see a smaller door without an apartment number next to the entrance to the other apartment. He put on a pair of latex gloves he had brought from his car and let himself into Wiegand's apartment, which was just a single room, plus a kitchen area and bathroom. Mihdí took a quick look through dresser drawers, but didn't find any evidence of spray-paint, gloves, or other relevant items, and there didn't seem to be any place to hide things like that, either. He made sure the apartment door locked behind him, then opened up the closet. There were clothes, a few games and some canned goods.

One of the shelves, though, was reserved for Wiegand's skinhead activities. There were flyers with racist rants. There were some DVDs that appeared to be distributed by neo-Nazi groups in the western United States. And there were four cans of black spray paint lined up on the shelf, along with an apparently unused pair of gloves. That wasn't a particularly helpful result, since Wiegand had just been caught with spray paint, but it did seem to confirm that Wiegand had prepared ahead of time, rather than simply purchasing spray paint on the spur of the moment. There were also two cans of red spray paint on the shelves as well, both of which seemed to be new and full.

Mihdí locked up the closet, returned the key to the owner and drove back to his office. He decided it might be helpful to do a bit of a brain mapping about the case. Using his favorite online brain-mapping site, he put the rabbi's name in the center. He then added the names of the key people he had talked to in the case. Several, such as Sam Schliebaum and Neil Hoffman, he moved to the side in a category of people without motives. Some of the others he placed under the boxes for people to whom they were connected, such as putting Rev. Crestwood under the box for Matthew Skefton. He annotated those whom he considered possible suspects with information about their character, motives, associates, and alibis. He didn't worry about making the brain map totally comprehensive, since it was only there to help him see where things stood.

Kurt Childs was at his desk nearby, so Mihdí called him over to look at the brain map. Greg Victor, another member of the detective squad, was in the office, so Mihdí invited him to join them as well. As they looked it over together, they could see that Mihdí had narrowed it down to four suspects: Scott Craig, Charlie Richardson, Matthew Skefton, and Brent Wiegand.

Kurt, who had been part of Mihdí's consultation earlier that day, noticed that Ahmad Muhammad was not one of them. "I know Beth thought he should be checked out," he said to Mihdí, "but I'm with you on this. He had nothing to do with it."

They looked at each of the four in turn.

"Just based on motive," Mihdí said, "I'd peg Richardson as having the strongest . . . what would you say . . . traditional motive. He could make a lot of money if his proposal were accepted, and it would be necessary for the synagogue to move for that to happen."

"But if I understand your notes properly," Greg observed, "he has an air-tight alibi."

Mihdí nodded.

"This Wiegand guy looks like pretty much a lowlife type," Greg said.

"I agree," said Kurt. "You've talked to him, right, Mihdí?"

"Yeah, I have," Mihdí replied. "More than once. He's a real piece of work. Bad attitude, bad history, bad beliefs. It seems reasonably likely he could be involved, although we have nothing specific tying him to the rabbi or the synagogue or even to Jews in general. His alibi is incomplete and unconfirmed, so he's definitely still in the frame."

"And Skefton?" Kurt asked.

"A bit of a wild card, I'd say," said Mihdí. "He certainly has the passion and seems to have had some kind of grudge against Klemme. But he's also a new Christian."

"Fanatical?" Kurt queried.

"Absolutely," Mihdí answered. "And he seems like he might be capable of murder under the right circumstances. But he'd also be worried about his eternal soul and would have some pretty significant hesitation about adding a mortal sin to his ledger."

"The stuff you have on this Scott Craig seems a bit sketchy," Greg said.

"Yes, I noticed that, too," said Kurt. "What's the story there?"

"Well, I tried to talk to him on Friday, but he had gone home sick. I have an appointment with him this afternoon, and I hope to tie up all of the loose ends. He's one of a group of young people in the synagogue, and I've only talked to a couple of them. It's possible one of the others will help fill in some gaps, too."

The three of them agreed that talking to Craig was top priority, then digging a bit deeper into Wiegand's past. They thought the other two suspects could wait.

* * *

Mihdí had lots of time before his scheduled appointment with Scott Craig, so he decided to try a consultation with some of the people involved

99

in the case. He drove up near the synagogue, which was only three minutes from the police station. He stopped in at Hoffman's Deli, HisStory Book Store, and ended up at Uncommon Brews, with Sandy Klarr, Neil Hoffman, and Harry Katz all in tow. They found a table and placed their orders, then they chatted until the coffees were served. Mihdí asked Ahmad Muhammad to join them.

"I know this is a bit unusual," he said to them all, "but it often helps me to consult with others about a case to see what perspectives I have missed and what facts I may have overlooked. I hope you're all open to the idea of talking things through a bit."

They all agreed, although there was a hefty degree of puzzlement spread around the table.

"I'd just like to have us work together to try to surface the truth. If you have a strong opinion about anything that comes up, just 'check it at the door,' as it were. For now, we just want to see what comes up when we talk about things."

"I wouldn't know where to start," said Sandy Klarr. "I don't even know much about the case."

"Well, let me fill you in on a few facts, but it's your fresh eyes that I'm counting on."

Mihdí went over the basic facts of the case, including the graffiti, the murder weapon, and the timing of events, as far as they were known. He didn't talk about any of the suspects, as that was confidential.

"So, given that very rough outline of what happened, let me ask you your general impressions."

"It still seems pretty obvious to me," ventured Harry Katz. "Somebody came to vandalize the place, and they offed the rabbi when he caught them at it."

"Wouldn't a vandal be much more likely to run than to commit murder?" asked Neil Hoffman. "Vandalism is a pretty low-level crime. It doesn't seem like a tagger would make such a quick jump to murder."

Sandy Klarr nodded her head in agreement and added, "I would think that it would be very difficult to commit murder. Taking a human life is a very bad thing to do, and I think everybody knows that. It's more than one giant step beyond vandalism."

"I guess you're right," said Katz. "But this wasn't just someone painting their name on the side of a boxcar, you know. It was a hate crime, and that's already a step or two beyond typical vandalism."

"Who would hate that much?" asked Ahmad. "In this country, it doesn't really seem like people have that much hate. Sometimes I see suspicion or fear in people when they see me, but not so much hate."

"So, what do you think would make anyone kill a rabbi, particularly one as generally respected and friendly as Jacob Klemme?" Mihdí asked the group.

"People do kill each other out of hate, don't they?" asked Sandy Klarr. "There were all those lynchings and stuff in the South years ago, right? Those were all basically hate crimes before they were called that."

"That's true," said Hoffman, "but it was almost always mob violence, not individual crimes. For individual murders, I would think you'd be more likely to look at love or money as motives, rather than some generalized hate. Once you've decided to kill someone, you may find it easier to do if you view the person as part of a group you hate. But hate, all by itself, is not gonna be enough to get you pull the trigger if you're looking at one particular person walking down the street, minding his own business."

"I'm not so sure about that," said Muhammad. "In some parts of the world, prejudice can be so strong that one group doesn't even view other groups as human. They can kill members of a different group without even feeling guilty because they think of it as killing an animal or digging up a weed in the garden."

Sandy Klarr winced at that idea. "Oh, that's terrible! How can society function when there are such prejudices and hatred?"

Nobody seemed to have an answer for that, so there was silence for a few moments.

"I think you're right, Ahmad," said Harry at length. "It may start with one group hating another, but maybe when one individual hater focuses his hatred on one other individual, he can feel justified in killing him just because he's considered as 'one of them.'"

Hoffman said, "I still think maybe love and money are much more likely to be motives. If somebody thinks somebody else is stealing their lover or if there's money to be made, that's when they'll get to the point of killing somebody."

"I think you need to mix the love motive with hatred," Harry speculated. "If somebody is stealing your lover, you're not going to be happy about it, but you don't kill them for that. The idea that somebody inferior is stealing your lover, though, might make your blood boil. I supposed that could apply to Rabbi Klemme if there was someone from a different religion who felt the rabbi had stolen someone from them, but I also think it would rule out a Jew. No Jew would think a rabbi as nice as Jacob could be inferior. Was he dating a non-Jew?"

"As far as I'm aware, Jacob's love life was completely within the Jewish community," Mihdí answered quietly.

"Then all we have left is money!" Harry stated triumphantly. He sat back in his chair as if the entire conversation were now over.

"Would there have to be something personal involved for money to be the motive," Mihdí asked, "or could that be completely impersonal?"

Neil Hoffman said, "How are we to know what moves someone to murder? I think it's a safe bet that none of us has ever seriously contemplated it, let alone gotten far enough along to experience what it might feel like."

"Is that a problem for the police, too, Detective Mongomery?" Sandy Klarr asked.

"Is what a problem?" Mihdí replied. "I'm not sure I get the question."

"Well, hopefully, none of the police have every committed murder, either," Sandy said. "How can you get inside the head of a murderer if you don't have any experience to tell you how a murderer thinks?"

"That's an interesting question, Montgomery," said Harry. "I've heard of the idea of police trying to think like criminals, but they can't really know how to do that, right?"

"Well, I hope that's right," Mihdí replied. "If we have any murderers in our ranks, I'm certainly not aware of them. But the same could be said for any type of psychology. People study psychology so they can learn things about the way people think and hopefully can apply the general principles of psychology even to other people's thoughts and motives that might seem quite foreign. It's certainly possible for us to feel empathy for people who have suffered things that we've never suffered."

"That's right," said Sandy. "Each of us has suffered in some way, whether it's from torture to stubbing our toes. We can translate our pain into empathy for those who have experienced far worse things than we have."

"I think this is a very important point," said Ahmad. "We all share parts of the human experience, so we can feel pain when our brothers and sisters feel pain, even if it's not directly affecting us."

Mihdí nodded and said, "Bahá'u'lláh, the Founder of the Bahá'í Faith tells us, '*Since We have created you all from one same substance it is incumbent on you to be even as one soul, to walk with the same feet, eat with the same mouth and dwell in the same land.*' I think He's talking about compassion, walking in somebody else's shoes."

"That's very beautiful, Detective," Sandy responded.

"Yes, I think so, too," Mihdí said. "But I'm afraid I've contributed to us getting hopelessly off topic."

Everyone laughed.

"I don't want you to think it's a total loss, though. I really gained a lot from this conversation," the detective said. "The way you talked through the possibilities and examined how each type of motive would play out was very helpful to me. I hope I haven't taken too much of your time."

Everyone got up and shook hands as they departed for their various shops. Mihdí paid for the coffees, embraced Ahmad, and went back to his car.

* * *

Mihdí drove over to Scott Craig's building and went up to the fifth floor office. He rang the bell on the receptionist's desk again, and the same woman who had helped him on his previous visit appeared a moment later.

"I have an appointment with Scott Craig," Mihdí said.

"I saw him come in earlier," the woman replied. "Let me go check on him."

Another woman came to the reception area a few minutes later.

"You're Detective Montgomery?" she asked.

"Yes, I am," Mihdí said. "And you are . . . ?"

"I'm Scott's secretary, Fang Yee," she said. "Scott's really busy today; he has a big deadline tomorrow. He was wondering if he could reschedule for another day."

"I don't think I can do that," Mihdí replied. "I want to see him now. Let him know that we can do it here, or I can arrange to have him taken in for questioning."

Fang Yee's eyes opened a bit wider, but she didn't react otherwise. "I'll give him the message," she said.

A few minutes later, Scott Craig emerged from the inner office area. Craig was short—no more than five foot seven—and had dark, curly hair. While he did not have facial hair, he had a very dark shadow of shaved whiskers on his chin and down his neck. His blue Oxford button-down shirt fit him perfectly, but the sleeves were rolled up, the top button was open, and his tie was loosened.

When Mihdi had first met Craig during the cleanup at the Beth Shalom synagogue, he had looked energized from all the manual labor they had done. Now, however he looked tired and harried. He said, "I'm sorry, Detective, I am very busy today. I hope this won't take long."

Mihdí just smiled and shrugged his shoulders. "We'll see," he said.

Craig nodded reluctantly and led Montgomery through the outer door to his office. Craig's desk was strewn with papers, and there were several documents open on the computer screen. Craig saw that Mihdí was looking at them, so he turned off his monitor with an angry flourish.

"Mr. Craig," Mihdí began. "Since you're busy, I'll get straight to the point. Did you kill Rabbi Klemme?"

"No!" Craig said, surprised. "Of course not!"

"If possible, I need you to prove that," Mihdí said. "You had an appointment with the rabbi at 6:00 p.m., and you notified the police shortly after that time. Can you account for your whereabouts during the rest of the afternoon?"

"Well, I can tell you what I did," Craig replied, "but I don't think I can prove anything to you."

"Let's start with that, then," said Mihdí.

"I was here all morning. I left at around 1:00 to go get lunch. I've had

something on my mind lately—a personal thing, so don't ask what it was—
and I was really torn up about it that day. I called Jacob to set up a time to see
him after work. But then I felt like I needed to do some thinking. So I drove
over to Pulaski Woods and just walked trails for a few hours. After that I went
home to wait to go to the synagogue at 6:00."

"And you didn't see anyone you knew in that time who could verify any
part of this?"

"No, I'm afraid I didn't, Detective. I didn't know I'd need an alibi."

"Of course," Mihdí said. "It's perfectly natural. It's just not very convenient for you."

"I'll agree with you there," replied Scott.

"When you were at home, did you use your computer or make phone calls
or anything that would show that you were there?"

Craig looked down in his lap and said, "No. I just read the newspaper and
flipped on the tube for a while."

Mihdí waited for a moment to see if Scott would say more, but he kept his
eyes down and stayed silent.

"OK then," Mihdí continued. "You've said that the subject of your appointment with Rabbi Klemme is off limits. I understand your desire for
privacy, and I suspect you won't tell me anything more now. I just want to
warn you that if the subject eventually appears to have some bearing on the
case, or if I feel there's some connection, I may need you to tell me more.
Would you like to tell me more at this point?"

"No," Craig said, looking up briefly.

"So noted," said Mihdí. "I'd like to ask you about your relationship with
Tamar Ornstein. Can you tell me about that?"

"There's not much to tell, really. We went out for a while, and then she
broke it off."

"When was that, exactly?"

"I don't know. About six months ago, maybe."

"Did she give a reason?"

"I think you should ask her that question," Scott snapped.

"I'd like to hear what you have to say about it."

"She said a lot of stuff, but I figured it boiled down to falling out of love."

105

"Did it have anything to do with Jacob Klemme?" Mihdí pursued.

"She mentioned that she had thought about him, but they didn't have any special relationship at that time."

"But she started one pretty soon after you two broke up, right?"

"I guess so."

"How did you feel about that?"

"I love Tammy. I mean I loved her. But I didn't have any claim on her. I just told her she had to do what she had to do."

"So you didn't bear a grudge against the rabbi?"

"No," Craig said crisply.

"But it would be perfectly natural for you to . . ." Mihdí began.

"Look," Scott interrupted, "I told you I didn't bear a grudge, and that's the end of it, OK? I wasn't happy about Tammy breaking up with me, but it wasn't Klemme's fault. He was a nice guy. I liked him. End of story."

Mihdí gave him a moment to settle down, then asked, "Can you tell me a bit about other young people at the Temple? Obviously there's you and Tammy, but who else?"

"Um, there's Judy David, Tammy's best friend, and Jesse and Sam Gutman, and Hannah Pollack. I can't think of any others right now. Those are the ones I know the best."

Mihdí decided he had gotten all that he was going to get from Craig for the time being. He wished him good day and returned to his car. He stopped in the office and found the names that Scott Craig had given him in the Beth Shalom directory that Sam Schliebaum had given him. He compared those names to the ones that Kurt Childs had already spoken to. He didn't think he'd learn too much from most of these people and decided not to follow up at that time. But he thought it might be useful to talk to Tammy Ornstein's friend, Judy David. He called the number listed for her and arranged to come to her home the next morning before Judy left for work. It was already after 5:00 by that time, so he headed home for the evening.

Following Andrea's family's tradition, the Montgomerys usually had just popcorn for dinner on Sunday evenings. It was an easy thing to fix, everybody liked it, and they could sit and eat it in the living room while watching a movie together. Since the previous night had been a Feast night, they had postponed their popcorn night until Monday. It was nearing the holiday season and eggnog was available at the supermarket, so they each had a small glass as an appetizer. Mihdí made the popcorn on the stove while Andrea got the kids bathed and in pajamas so they could go straight to bed when the time came. They inserted a movie into the DVD player and sat back and watched while eating their popcorn. After Andrea and Mihdí put the kids to bed, they finished the popcorn and chatted until their own bedtime.

Tuesday, Day 7

After dropping off Enoch at school and Lua at her daycare, Mihdí drove to Judy David's house to keep their appointment. She lived in University Park, about a half-hour drive from Pine Bluff. She answered her door immediately and ushered Mihdí into her living room. As he was sitting down, she offered him a cup of coffee.

"That's very kind of you, Ms. David, but I gave up caffeine some years ago. If I had some now, I would probably stay awake for a week."

"I have some herbal teas if you'd like."

"No, thank you, I'm fine."

"I'll get some for myself, if you don't mind."

"Please, make yourself at home," Mihdí joked. They both laughed.

When she had gotten her coffee, she sat down in an easy chair facing Mihdí.

"I talked to that young detective last week," she began.

"Yes, I know. Detective Childs. I saw his notes. I don't know if there's anything to add to what you said then, but sometimes I get different ideas just from hearing things myself. Have you been a member of Beth Shalom for a long time?"

"You could say that. My parents attended when I was growing up, so I went along."

"Do your parents still go?"

"No. My Dad was killed in an industrial accident six years ago. Mom was from out east originally, so after Dad's death, she moved back to New Jersey.

Her parents are there, and she's able to look in on them and do things for them now and then since she's close by."

"Have you been attending regularly since childhood?"

"No. I'd come sometimes, like during the High Holy Days and things like that, but I wasn't regular until just recently. Tammy told me about Jacob and how cool he was, and I started coming most weeks since then."

"Do you think you'll keep going now that . . . ?"

"I will for a while at least. Tammy's really broken up about Jacob, of course, and she has lots of friends in the congregation. We've both been finding it fulfilling being more observant, so I think it will be good for both of us to keep going."

"That's very thoughtful and kind of you. Have you and Tammy been friends a long time?"

"Yep. Her parents were members at Beth Elohim in Joliet for a while, but they left there after some kind of row with the congregation. Tammy and I knew each other from Hebrew school and other stuff, so when her family started coming to Beth Shalom, we became best friends. We were probably around fourteen then. She didn't attend regularly until just recently, either, although she came more than I did. She lives as far north from Pine Bluff as I live south, but we both work in Midlothian for the same company. We're in different departments, but we see each other just about every day."

"Oh, I didn't know that. Did you see her last Tuesday?"

"Oh, yeah. That was the day she and Scott got into it at her office."

"Oh, right," said Mihdí, deftly covering his surprise. "Tell me about that."

"Well, she and Jacob were going to announce their engagement over the weekend, so she gave Scott a call that morning to let him know, so he wouldn't be blindsided."

"Tammy and Jacob were engaged?"

"Well, it was under wraps so far. They were going to make it official on the weekend. Anyway, at lunchtime, Scott came over and was trying to talk Tammy out of it. She told him to leave, and he started shouting at her. He's got a bit of a temper sometimes. Eventually, he left, but Tammy got in trouble for disturbing everybody anyway. And it wasn't her fault. It was so unfair!"

"It sounds a bit unfair, doesn't it?"

"Tammy told me all about it that afternoon when we had coffee together. But she hasn't really talked about it since then. In fact, I asked her about it the other day, and she didn't really answer me; she changed the subject or something."

"So you don't know any more details?"

"I think I've told you pretty much everything I know about it."

"Tell me more about Tammy and Scott's relationship."

"Hmm. Well, they've known each other since they were children. They had already kissed before I met Tammy, when she was fourteen. They had periods of hot and cold, I guess, but really they were always a couple. They had talked about marriage, but neither of them seemed in a hurry about it. They'd been engaged for about a year when Tammy broke it off, but they'd never set a wedding date."

"Interesting. How were they together?"

"I don't know. I never felt that Scott was all that special. He's really into football, and he works like twelve hours a day, so they didn't spend all that much time together. And he has a really short fuse. He'd blow up at the drop of a hat. Scared me. I didn't try to talk Tammy out of marriage with him, but I can't say I was particularly encouraging, either."

"And Tammy's relationship with Jacob?"

"That was pretty different. Tammy and I haven't spent as much time together recently because she was with him. They had dinner together often, and she'd go early to Temple to help set up and would stay late sometimes. They saw each other a lot on Sundays. When we had lunch or break together, she talked about him all the time."

"A bit more spark there, then, eh?"

"Definitely. They were just ready to announce their engagement, and I think they probably would have gotten married sometime next year. They were looking at possibilities for May and June."

"Since you, Tammy, and Scott all attended Temple together, you must have seen Scott and Jacob interact at some point."

"I suppose so. Scott kept his distance from Jacob when he could. He was courteous, you know, but not friendly. More than once, I thought that he kept coming so he could keep an eye on Tammy."

"Any other thoughts?"

"Not really."

Mihdí stood up. "I think I've got what I need. I really appreciate you taking the time to talk to me. I hope I didn't make you late for work."

"I don't go in until one today."

Judy walked Mihdí to the door, and they shook hands before he left.

*   *   *

Mihdí sat in his car for a few minutes trying to make up his mind whether to talk to Scott Craig or Tammy Ornstein first. Tammy had downplayed her relationship with Klemme, while Judy had said that they were planning to announce their engagement. Tammy certainly had not mentioned her call to Scott about the upcoming engagement announcement and had apparently lied to Mihdí when she said she hadn't spoken to Craig or seen him for a few weeks. And neither Scott nor Tammy had mentioned their argument to him, so he would have to follow up with both of them. He decided that they must have agreed to keep this quiet to try to protect Craig from the suspicion that would naturally fall on him. It made sense to him to talk to Tammy first so he would have more information when he talked to Scott. He checked his phone for directions and started driving towards Midlothian, where he hoped to find Tammy at work.

He had just started driving when he got a phone call. He saw that it was from Kurt Childs, so he pulled over to the side of the road and answered it.

"Mihdí," Childs said, "I just got transferred a call from Ahmad Muhammad at the coffee shop. He says there's someone there you need to talk to urgently."

"He didn't give any more details?"

"Nope. Ahmad wanted to talk to you, but he agreed to talk to me when they said you were out. But he wouldn't tell me any more than that. Do you want me to go over there?"

"No, I can go. I'm about a half hour away, but I'm already in the car. I'll give you a call once I get there if I need your help."

"Sure thing, Mihdí. Good luck."

112

Mihdí changed course and headed back towards Pine Bluff. As expected, it took him about half an hour to get to Uncommon Brews.

When Mihdí entered the shop, he greeted Ahmad in Arabic, "As-salamu alaykum!"

Ahmad Muhammad smiled and gave the appropriate response, "Wa alaykumu as-salam!"

They shook hands, and Ahmad asked Mihdí about Mihdí's health. Mihdí answered politely and asked about Ahmad's health in return. They exchanged a few sentences about their families, and Ahmad asked how the investigation was going. Mihdí told him he was pursuing several lines of inquiry and left it at that. He asked Ahmad how his business was going and whether the worsening weather was affecting it. Mihdí knew enough about Arab culture to recognize that this exchange of pleasantries and news took precedence over the urgency of the phone call, so he waited until Ahmad brought up the reason for the call.

"I would like you to meet my cousin, Hamdi, Detective," said Ahmad after the traditional greeting ritual had been observed. "He's one of my suppliers, and he is in the back, stocking some shelves." Ahmad led Mihdí to the cramped back room, but nobody was there. They proceeded through the open back door to the alley behind the shop. A delivery van was parked there, and a man was rearranging some supplies in the back of the truck.

"Hamdi!" Ahmad called.

The man turned around and smiled. He hopped down out of the truck.

"This is the detective I was telling you about, Hamdi," Ahmad said. "Mihdí Montgomery."

Mihdí extended his hand, and the other man shook it.

"This is Hamdi Sellimi," Ahmad continued. "He is married to my uncle's—my father's sister's husband's—sister. His company supplies disposable goods for shops like mine all around the south suburbs."

"I'm very pleased to make your acquaintance," Mihdí said.

"Please," said Ahmad, "let's go inside and talk."

The three of them filed through the back room and back into the coffee shop proper. Ahmad insisted that his two friends sit down, while he made them all some coffee. There were no other customers at that moment, so they could speak privately.

"Decaf cappuccino for you, Detective?" Ahmad called over as Mihdí sat down.

"Yes, thanks! Good memory."

Ahmad smiled and nodded.

Hamdi Sellimi, like Ahmad Muhammad, was thin but not tall. Despite his thinness, or perhaps because of it, the powerful muscles of his arms and legs were apparent. While Ahmad was making the coffees, Mihdí chatted with Ahmad's "cousin." He could tell that the Tunisian understood only about half of what Mihdí said to him, but Sellimi had a sunny smile that remained on his face no matter what. He seemed excited to be helping the police on a case. Despite Sellimi's poor English, Mihdí learned a bit about his business and tried to straighten out the relationship between him and Ahmad. They were still working on that when Ahmad joined them.

"What's this about, Ahmad?" Mihdí asked.

"I was telling Hamdi about the rabbi's murder and the ongoing investigation you're conducting. He hadn't heard anything about it, since he lives in . . . Where is it you live, cousin?"

"Harvey," Hamdi answered.

"Tell him the story, Hamdi."

Hamdi turned to the detective. "I am come here on Tuesdays, like last Tuesday. Since Ahmad my cousin, I am stay here longer. Last week I am moving things around in my truck. Young guy come out of back door that way." He pointed in the direction away from the synagogue.

"It was the bookstore," Ahmad said. "Hamdi showed me earlier."

"He walk down alleyway past me. Not see me. Pass truck, and I am not see where he go. I am get last load for Ahmad and get off truck. Same guy run out of Jew house. Run back to his door—bookstore?" Ahmad nodded to confirm this.

"Can you describe this man, Mr. Sellimi?"

"Young, twenty? Wear red shirt. Long sleeve. Light hair."

"You said a red shirt?"

Hamdi nodded. "Dark red."

"You say he ran out of the synagogue back to the bookstore? Did you see his face? Did he look scared or angry or happy or . . . ?"

"Scared, maybe. No, maybe angry." He shrugged. "Don't know."

"How long would you say he was in the synagogue?"

"Few minutes. Not more."

"Do you happen to know what time all of this happened?"

"Three, maybe. Ten after, maybe."

"Did you notice anything else about him?"

Hamdi shook his head.

"Well," said Mihdí, "this is very helpful information. Ahmad, thanks for calling me. I'm sure it will make a big difference."

Mihdí got Hamdi's contact information so he could call him back if he had more questions.

*   *   *

Although Mihdí felt that he needed to follow up quickly on the new information he had received about Scott Craig earlier that morning, he was closer to the HisStory bookstore, so he decided to interrogate Matthew Skefton again. He looked into the store window and saw that Skefton was there. He called Kurt Childs and asked him to meet him there with a few officers.

Mihdí entered the store without waiting for the others to arrive. There were no other customers inside, and Skefton was putting new stock out on the shelves. Skefton got up to greet his customer but frowned when he saw who it was.

"Sorry to bother you again, Mr. Skefton, but I was just wondering if you had remembered anything else about the day of the rabbi's murder."

Matthew stared at him for a few seconds. He seemed to be processing Mihdí's sudden appearance in the bookstore and considering how he should answer. Finally he said, "Nope."

"What was it that caused you not to like Rabbi Klemme, Matthew? I understand that he helped keep you out of court."

Matthew looked at him with some surprise but didn't ask how Mihdí had learned that. "I guess. I had to do all the work. He just did a lot of talking."

"And do I also recall correctly that he was the one who suggested you find a church?"

115

"He might have said something like that. But he was a Jew, so he must of had some reason for telling me that."

"Yes, I'm sure he had a reason. Probably that he cared about you. But why didn't you like him?"

"I didn't trust him. He didn't make sense, and he acted like I owed him somethin' but I didn't owe him nothin.'"

"Okay. When did you say you last saw him?"

"I don't remember. I think it was a few days before he was killed."

"So, when you went to the synagogue last Tuesday, you didn't see him?"

Matthew stared at him. "What do you mean? I ain't never been in that place."

"Matthew, I have an eyewitness who puts you in the synagogue during the time period when the murder took place. Start answering my questions truthfully, and I can determine whether I need to arrest you right now. Tell me about going to the synagogue on Tuesday."

Skefton walked to the counter and sat down behind it, with Mihdí following very close behind. Mihdí took a chair as well. Skefton avoided returning the detective's gaze, mostly staring at his feet. He was obviously reluctant to talk, but knew he was backed into a corner.

"My church wants to find a new building, 'cause we're gettin' too big for our current place. I thought that Temple might be a good spot, if the Jews cleared out of it. I just wanted to look around a little and see for myself."

"That sounds reasonable enough."

"So, I went over there after I had my lunch. I went in the back door, because I thought I could kinda sneak in and not be seen. There was some offices and restrooms and stuff like that back there. No sanctuary. So I kept walking. Then I looked in another door, and Klemme was sitting there at a desk, doing something on the computer. I don't think he saw me, but I didn't want to talk to him. I high-tailed it out of there and ran back here. I didn't kill him. He was alive when I left."

"That sounds like a plausible story, Matthew, but I'll need to check out a few facts. In the meantime, I'm going to need you to come down to the station and make a formal statement."

Detective Childs and the officers he had arranged to come arrived a few minutes later. Mihdí called Stephanie Plante, and Mihdí allowed Skefton to wait until she arrived before they took him in. He even allowed Skefton to serve a pair of customers who came in during that time. With waiting for Stephanie to arrive, then talking with her a bit, it was pushing noon by the time the detectives, officers, and Matthew finally arrived at the station. Mihdí had requested that Matthew come in of his own free will so he would not need to arrest him. He observed Kurt Childs take Matthew's statement, then talked briefly to Skefton while the statement was being typed up for him to sign. The young man was obviously rattled, but Mihdí's calming influence helped to keep him from freaking out too much. All told, dealing with Skefton took almost three hours. When it was all wrapped up, Mihdí had an officer drive Matthew back to the bookstore. Then he went out to get a bit of a snack to tide him over until dinnertime.

Mihdí was being perfectly honest in saying that Skefton's story was plausible, but he recalled his conversation with Stephanie Plante, who thought he was capable of murder. Given the account given by Ahmad's relative, Hamdi Sellimi, it did not seem that Matthew would have had time to do all of the graffiti while he was in the synagogue. But if he had come to the synagogue just after the rabbi had surprised and scared away a vandal, it looked to Mihdí that it would have been possible for him to find the candelabra and murder the rabbi, all in the name of finding a proper home for his church. He certainly was not yet ready to drop Skefton from his investigation.

* * *

Mihdí called Tammy Ornstein to verify that she was at work that day, then drove over to Midlothian to her office. She met him in the lobby and escorted him to a private conference room near the rear of the office.

When they were both seated, Mihdí said, "I had a chat with your friend, Judy, this morning."

Tammy nodded, "Yes, she told me you were coming over."

"I just need to clarify a few points that came up in my conversation with her."

Tammy nodded again, but did not speak.

"She told me that Scott Craig had come to your office last Tuesday and tried to talk you out of getting engaged to Jacob. I need to ask about that because there are a number of discrepancies with what you told me when I first talked to you. Would you like to tell me what really happened this time?"

Tammy looked down and clasped and unclasped her hands nervously. Her breath was shallow and strained as if she was struggling to control it. She took a deep breath and lifted her head to face Mihdí.

"I'm sorry that I didn't tell you about all that before. I was afraid that Scott might have done something bad, and I wanted to protect him."

"Understandable, but it still counts as obstruction. Let's clear it up now."

"Jacob and I were going to announce our engagement last weekend. I knew Scott still had the idea that he and I would end up together eventually. Jacob thought that it would be considerate to give Scott a call to let him know ahead of time so he would be emotionally prepared for the public announcement. I called Scott on Tuesday morning and told him about it. He didn't say much, but I could tell he was upset and angry. Actually, I knew before I called him that he'd be upset and angry. He has quite a temper sometimes."

"I've heard that from others as well."

"Anyway, I was glad I had done it, because I didn't want to have to see him at services and get into it there. I had some meetings to prepare for in the afternoon, so I just concentrated on that and put Scott out of my mind. But then he showed up here a little after noon. I think I told you I had meetings from noon on, but they actually only started at 1:00 p.m. I didn't really want to talk to Scott, but he didn't give me much choice. I didn't want to make it easy for him by going into a conference room or something, and honestly, I was a bit afraid of what he might say if we were alone, so we just stayed at my desk. He talked to me for quite a while, telling me that he still loved me and that he wanted me to reconsider marrying Jacob. He said he thought I wouldn't be happy and that he could make me happier. He even brought up a few stories about when we were younger and some of the fun times we had. I do like Scott, and we have had lots of good times together. We laughed at some of the stories, and I even told a few of my own.

"But after we had talked maybe half an hour, I told him quite clearly that I was still going to marry Jacob. He sort of begged me a little bit, but I didn't budge. After a while, he started to get angry. It wasn't too bad at first, but when I tried to get him to calm down, that just made him angrier. Eventually, he was yelling at me and swearing and calling me and Jacob names."

She paused for a moment. "He said he'd kill Jacob. Of course, I didn't believe him. He's threatened to kill just about everybody he knows at one time or another, including me. It's just something he says, you know? One of the other people here called security because of the uproar. But after he blew his stack at me, Scott stormed out of the office. I don't know what he did then, but he was angrier than I had ever seen him."

"Did you talk to him again that day?"

"No, I didn't see him, and he didn't call after that. I certainly wasn't going to call him. But he called me at home on Wednesday morning. He asked if I had heard about Jacob, which I had—Jacob's mother had called me Tuesday night, after the police had contacted her about it. He told me he was the one who discovered Jacob at the synagogue. Then he said that he was worried that the police would misinterpret his outburst and think that he had done it. He asked me to say I hadn't talked to him for a while. Scott's not capable of killing anybody, so I believed him. I didn't want to lie, but I knew it wouldn't look good for him, so I agreed."

Mihdí waited a while before speaking, to see if she had more to say. When it was clear she had finished, he said, "Thank you for giving me all of that information. Things would have been far easier if I had known these details when I first talked to you. If Scott is innocent, as you believe, the facts will clear him. If he's guilty, you will be charged with obstruction of justice. Do you understand?"

Tammy nodded her understanding and began to cry.

"I'll take my leave, Ms. Ornstein. Please give me a call if you think of anything else that you think has any bearing on this case. I would appreciate it if you would keep our conversation entirely to yourself, and I would particularly ask you not to talk to Scott Craig until I have a chance to interview him."

She nodded and was still sobbing quietly as he left the conference room and made his way out of the office to his car.

* * *

It was coming up on 5:00 by the time Mihdí got back to the office. He still needed to verify Matthew Skefton's story. Skefton's minister, Rev Elijah Crestwood, had given Mihdí his cell number, so Mihdí gave him a call.

"Crestwood," the voice on the other end said. "Who is this?"

"It's Detective Montgomery, pastor. I wondered if you could answer a few quick questions."

"I'm at work, Detective, but if it doesn't take too long, it shouldn't be a problem."

"Great, thank you. I was speaking to Matthew Skefton earlier today, and he said that the church was hoping to move to a new location. Do I have that right?"

"Yes, sir," the minister responded. "We have a storefront church in Romeoville which we're starting to outgrow. We're not desperate, but we would love to find the right place. If we expand much more, we will definitely need a larger building."

"Would you consider moving the church to Pine Bluff?" Mihdí followed up.

"Oh, yes. That would be great. We have a few members from Pine Bluff itself, plus we have a number of people that come from east of there, and that would reduce their trips."

"Did the subject of the Beth Shalom synagogue building ever come up between you and Matthew?"

"Now that you mention it, yes. He said there was a synagogue near the store where he works. He said he hadn't been inside but that it looked like it might be a good location for our church, if the Jews happened to leave. Matthew told me a few weeks ago that he was going to try to get over there and see it so he could tell me more."

"Did he report back that he had done so?"

"No. I assume he hasn't had a chance to get over there yet."

Mihdí thanked Crestwood for the information and ended the call.

Kurt Childs was in the office, so Mihdí went to his desk to talk things over. He told Childs all of the developments related to Scott Craig and asked his thoughts about him.

"Well, that all does seem to add up to something, doesn't it? But his ex said she didn't think he was capable of murder, right?"

"Yeah, that's right."

"Doesn't mean much, of course. Nobody seems capable of murder until they actually do it."

"That was my thought, too. You've spoken to him. Do you think he's likely to be a flight risk or to do something else violent or dangerous?"

"He might, if he gets angry. You said he's a bit prone, right? Personally, I'd worry about leaving him another day. Do you want me to have him brought in?"

Mihdí thought it over for a minute, then said, "No, I think not. I don't know that there's anybody else left for him to be that angry with. I told Tammy Ornstein not to talk to him. I'd like to know more about his movements and such after he talked to her last Tuesday before I confront him, but I don't know if that's going to be possible. He seems to be carrying on pretty normally for now. I think it can wait for tomorrow."

"Your decision, boss. I hope you're right."

Mihdí went back to his office, shut down his computer, grabbed his coat, and left for the day.

* * *

After the kids had gone to bed that night, Mihdí was completely distracted by his case, but he sat in the living room attempting to read while Andrea worked at the computer.

Andrea broke the brief silence. "I just got an e-mail from Brenda. She has agreed to be the Bahá'í reader at the Interfaith Thanksgiving service tomorrow."

"Oh, that's good," Mihdí said. "I did it last year, didn't I?"

"Yes," Andrea replied. "And the year before as well, I think. I knew you didn't want to do it again, and I've done it a few times myself, so the Assembly asked Brenda to do it this time. She seems happy to have been asked."

"That's great," Mihdí said. "I'm sure she'll do a good job."

They settled into silence again for a few minutes.

She asked him, "Are you going to be able to go with us to Mom and Dad's for Thanksgiving on Thursday, honey?" she asked Mihdí.

"I really don't know," he said. "I'm not sure there's much of anything I can do on Thanksgiving to move this case along, but if I don't get a break pretty soon, it feels like it might slip through my fingers completely. I don't really know where to go from here."

"You should pray about it," his wife said. "Just open your heart to God, and let Him give you guidance. The worst thing that could happen is that you'll be in the same place you are now."

"That's a good idea, sweetheart. I'm going to go into the family room and give it a go."

Mihdí put a cushion on the floor, sat down, leaned against the couch, and read some prayers from his Bahá'í prayer book. Then he tried to clear his mind and open himself up to God's guidance. Mihdí didn't think of himself as being "good at prayer." He prayed every day and always felt that it was a good use of his time, and he usually felt that his prayers were answered in subtle ways that he was able to recognize after a few hours, days, or years had passed. Sometimes he wished God would take more of a direct approach to answering his prayers, but on this night, he was so unsettled he felt that even subtle guidance was better than none. He concentrated first on his breathing, then repeated a phrase from one of the prayers over and over in his mind: *"O God, guide me."* His main concern was to get away from conscious thought about the case. He wanted to clear the slate so God could write on it if He so chose. Whenever a thought came into his head, he tried to just notice it and return to his repeated phrase.

After about twenty minutes, a new thought came into Mihdí's head: "Why now?" It was a very simple thought, just a little question, but it seemed in his mind as if it were related to the case. Mihdí noticed the thought and acknowledged it, then returned to repeating the phrase. But this time, the thought did not go away. He decided this was a signal that his concentration had reached its limit, and he got up.

Andrea had gone to bed, so he went up and joined her there.

She was still awake, reading a book. "How did it go, sweet thing?" she asked.

"I'm not sure," Mihdí said as he undressed and got ready for bed. "I'll think about it more in the morning."

She was used to him keeping things to himself, so she didn't press it.

Mihdí got into bed and immediately felt his eyelids grow heavy as he lay down against his pillow. The room was quiet, and the sound of Andrea turning a page every so often was relaxing, so he was soon asleep.

Wednesday, Day 8

In the morning, as they got ready for the day, Andrea asked Mihdí again about his experience with asking God for assistance the night before. "Do you feel any different now?"

He told her about the thought that had come into his head: "Why now?"

"Do you have any idea what it means?" she asked him.

Mihdí finished tying his tie and putting on the jacket of his dark suit before answering. "Well, it's usually a good question to ask in an investigation and one I haven't yet focused on this time," he replied. "If this was premeditated murder—or even if it wasn't, I guess—there may be some reason why it happened when it did and not a week or month before or after. I think it might be worth having another consultation session about it."

"Or even just thinking about it on your own," she suggested. "In any case, it seems like there's at least a possibility that it could be an answer to your prayer, so don't ignore it."

Mihdí was slightly irritated that she would think he might, but he just forced a smile and said, "I won't, honey. I'll work on it today."

When Mihdí arrived at Pine Bluff Police Headquarters, he went to the briefing room, where the morning briefing was just breaking up. He located Beth Carr, Kurt Childs, and Greg Victor and beckoned them to join him.

"Do you all have a minute?"

"Yeah, of course, Mihdí. What's up?"

"Do you still remember most of the details of the consultation we had the other day about the rabbi's murder? That's the case where you were looking at the brain map on my computer, Greg."

"Mind like a steel trap, Detective," said Beth Carr, as the others nodded.

"I don't want to tell you why I'm asking, I just want you to consider a question."

"OK," said Beth. "You're nothing if not mysterious, Detective."

"If the most important question in this case was, 'Why now?', who would you think of as the prime suspect?"

Beth was intrigued. "Interesting. Let me think a second. There are the four guys: the bookstore guy, the ex, the real estate guy, and the Muslim coffee guy, right?"

Kurt Childs broke in, "Nah, Ahmad Muhammad had nothing to do with it. I'd stake my reputation on it."

Mihdí chuckled. "I agree. You've always considered him as a possible suspect, but I've never thought so, and I still don't. The fourth one is the skinhead guy, Brent Wiegand."

"Oh, yeah." After a few more moments of thought, she said, "I can only really talk about three of them. We didn't know much about the ex—uh, Craig wasn't it? So I can't really say anything about him. But of the three I know something about, I'd say that Charlie guy, the real estate dude, has a clear motive. He could make a lot of money from this, and there was some time pressure on that deal, right?"

"Yeah, that's right. Kurt and Greg, what do you think?"

Greg Victor said, "From what I remember, it seemed like most of the questions in the case were about the ex-boyfriend. I'd vote for him."

"You're right about that," Kurt said. "And I don't know everything you've found out about him since then, Mihdí, so I'd agree with Greg on that. But since you asked specifically about the question 'Why now?', I'd lean more towards Richardson."

"That was my conclusion as well, but I wanted to consult with others about it, because it's easy to get lost in a sea of facts."

"Have you gotten any new information that damages his alibi?" Kurt asked.

Mihdí shook his head, "Nope, nothing. It would be a stretch to see how he could have done it. I just wanted to explore that particular question a bit more."

126

"So, what's this about?" Beth asked. "Do you have some new evidence or something that makes you want to focus on that question?"

"Let's just say your help could be an answer to prayer." Mihdí smiled enigmatically and left the three of them with puzzled looks on their faces.

With the next day being Thanksgiving, Mihdí thought he should work through quite a few leads before the holiday made too many people unavailable. He wanted to talk again to Brent Wiegand. And, while he didn't have any good explanation available for how Charlie Richardson could have been involved in the murder, he thought it wouldn't hurt to talk to him again, particularly given the others' response to the question from his prayer.

But he knew he definitely needed to talk to Scott Craig, so he called Craig's cell phone and got a very sleepy "Hello?" in response. It turned out that Scott had taken the day off and was leaving around noon to visit his parents in Rockford for the Thanksgiving holiday. Mihdí arranged to come to Craig's house at 11:00.

The next call was to the Bridgeview Police Department to check on Brent Wiegand. Wiegand had been released pending trial, so Mihdí tried calling him at home. He picked up and said he didn't have to work that day. Mihdí said he had a few questions and would stop by on his way to Scott Craig's house.

Finally, Mihdí called the Richardson Real Estate and Development office and found that Charlie Richardson was expected any moment but would be out of the office most of the day. Mihdí told the receptionist that he'd be right over and went down to his car. Richardson's office was only about five minutes away, so Mihdí got there a bit after nine. Mihdí could hear Richardson on the phone in his office, so the detective waited in the outer office for a few minutes. Mihdí heard Richardson hang up, so he headed towards Richardson's door, and the two of them almost bumped into one another.

"Ah, Ximena said you were going to drop by. What can I do for you, Detective?"

Mihdí began, "I wanted to ask you about the city's big redevelopment plan, Mr. Richardson. I understand you have been developing a proposal for partnering in the project."

"Yes," Richardson said. "It could be a very lucrative deal, and I'd love to be able to get in on the action."

"How would you rate your chances at this point," Mihdí asked him.

"I tell you what, Detective Montgomery," Richardson answered with a slightly irritated edge in his voice. "I'd be happy to fill you in on the whole project and where I might fit into it, but I really don't have the time right now. I'm meeting some people—actually it's the Grants, that same couple we talked about last time—up at the north end of town at 9:30, and I don't want to be late. They seem like good prospects for a sale, and I don't want them to walk. I need the business in this market."

Mihdí did a quick mental calculation to decide whether this latest excuse from Richardson was simply an attempt to block the course of his investigation, but he decided that there wasn't really much to go on besides his gut feeling.

"I get that," he told the real estate agent. "I talked to the Grants last week, and they said they were meeting you. I won't keep you. Tomorrow's Thanksgiving, but perhaps we can talk again on Friday?"

"That might work," Richardson said. "I've got a few appointments with folks throughout the weekend, but my schedule's not full by any means. Would 1:00 p.m. work for you on Friday?"

"I should be able to do that, yes," Mihdí said. "Thanks for your time, Mr. Richardson."

*   *   *

Mihdí had not yet received the murder investigation file from the New Lenox police department for the previous murder—the one for which Brent Wiegand had been questioned—so he decided he would try to get something out of Wiegand himself about it. Getting to Wiegand's apartment took only a few minutes. He went around to the side and up the stairs and knocked on Wiegand's door. When Wiegand opened the door, he was wearing only a pair of boxer shorts. He didn't greet Mihdí; he merely turned and walked back to the couch, where he plopped down and crossed his arms.

"Thanks for seeing me, Mr. Wiegand. I just have a few things I'd like to talk over with you."

No response.

"I understand that you were questioned about six months ago about a murder in New Lenox. Can you tell me about that?"

Wiegand started a bit, but didn't respond immediately. Mihdí waited in silence.

"I was at a bar, drinkin' with some friends after work one day. I ain't got a car, so I was just walking around trying to find the train station when I left. When they found that dude's body, some folks reported having seen me around there. The cops tracked me down through the bar and picked me up. I told 'em I ain't had nothin' to do with it. They kept me there for a while, but they didn't have nothin' to tie me to no murder, so they let me go."

"And was that the last of it, or did you talk to the police again after that?"

"Not until you showed up here."

"Okay. Why were you drinking in New Lenox, if I can ask?"

"My buddy, Jason, lives over there. He's ex-Army, so that VFW post is his normal hangout. We go over there sometimes."

"Mmm. I'd like to ask you about the night you were arrested at the Islamic Center in Bridgeview. Tell me about that."

"Well, I just decided to go over there to mess the place up, so I did."

"Why did you pick that place?"

"Just felt like it. No reason."

"The literature I found in your hall storage closet was all about African Americans, not about Muslims, so why did you target the Islamic Center?"

"I told ya, no reason."

"When you were arrested, you were wearing gloves. Why was that?"

"I didn't want to leave fingerprints, you moron! Why else? I didn't expect to git caught, did I?

"Those gloves had quite a bit of fresh black paint on them. That's the color you were using to spray slogans on the wall there, so that makes sense. But they also had red paint on them, and I found some cans of red spray paint in your storage closet. How did your gloves get the red paint on them?"

"Well, it's not the first time I used spray paint, is it?"

"Isn't it? Where else have you used it?"

"I don't remember. It was too long ago."

"Really? Those gloves looked pretty new to me. Are you sure if we checked with retailers that we wouldn't find that you bought them recently?"

"No, you wouldn't."

"How do you know they wouldn't remember?"

"Because I took a couple pairs from work. It's no big deal. They got thousands of 'em."

"But it was recently, right?"

"Mebbe."

"So you would remember where you used the red paint?"

"Just somewhere, alright!"

"No, it's not alright. If you vandalized some other place 'for no reason,' I want to know where it was."

"I'm not tellin' you. It's a secret."

"A secret? Between you and who else?"

"Nobody. Just me."

"But you did vandalize somewhere else?"

"I said, I'm not sayin' another word about it!"

Mihdí could see Wiegand was a bit rattled, so he pressed on with more questions.

"How did you know about the Islamic Center?"

"I didn't. I just was out and stumbled onto it."

"So, you just walked from here over to Bridgeview, picked a place at random, and it happened to be the Islamic Center? Is that it?"

"No, I didn't walk from here. I took the bus."

"In the middle of the night, you packed up your spray paint and gloves, took probably two or more buses for what must have taken more than an hour to a nowhere section of Bridgeview and just happened to find an Islamic Center? Come on, Brent, give me something I have at least a chance of believing!"

Wiegand sat silently, with his arms still crossed, glaring at Mihdí. Mihdí just sat, with as open a look as he could manage, waiting for Brent to speak. After more than a minute, Wiegand finally looked away and snorted.

"I went there on purpose. I got a ride from a friend at about midnight and just hung out until it was time."

"Until it was time? A specific time?"

"Yeah, I was supposed to wait until 3:30 in the morning."

"Supposed to wait until 3:30? Whose idea was that?"

Wiegand was sweating and his glance darted around nervously. "I mean I decided I would wait until then."

"Mmm. But that's not what you said. You said you were supposed to wait until 3:30. You wouldn't say that if you had planned it yourself. Whose plan was it?"

"I'm not sayin' nothin' more."

"Well, listen, Brent. You've already been arrested for vandalism. Because of the previous suspicion, you're unlikely to get off too easily. I think, in time, we can tie you to the spray paint at the synagogue, which puts you in line for at least manslaughter, if not first degree murder. If you're protecting someone by your silence, you might want to ask yourself if the consequences for you won't be worse this way."

Wiegand looked around like a trapped animal, breathing hard and rocking back and forth a bit on the couch.

"I can't tell you, man. I just can't."

Mihdí waited to see if Brent would go on, but he didn't.

"OK. I can see you're scared, and you've said you can't tell me anything more about that. But let me just go through a possible scenario. I won't even ask you to tell me if I'm right. Just keep looking me in the eyes."

Wiegand nodded and looked at Mihdí.

"Somebody has something over you, and you know precisely what it is and what it means. They have threatened you in some way—with exposure or harm or something—and they said you'd better obey their instructions or else. They told you to go to the Islamic Center at exactly 3:30am, break in, and vandalize the place."

Mihdí could see from Wiegand's expression that he was on the mark.

"Let me step back a pace or two with this. This same blackmailer told you last week to go to the synagogue and spray slogans there, right? You didn't feel like you had any choice, so you did it. But then the rabbi showed up and you didn't want to get caught, so you killed him."

"No way, man! I didn't see nobody."

"That's not what the evidence says. There were traces of spray paint on the rabbi's body, which means that some of it was done after the rabbi was killed."

131

"I don't know nuthin' about that. The note told me to leave the spray paint in the building. I sprayed what he asked, and then I left."

"You wrote three phrases on the wall?"

"Nah, man, just two, just like the note told me to do. Somethin' about Palestine and 'Death to the Jews.'"

"Brent, let's imagine that I believe your story. I can't help you if you don't tell me who is blackmailing you. It's likely you'll take the blame for the murder if we can't find somebody else to pin it on. Did they tell you that the reason you got arrested was that a tip was called in to the Bridgeview police that night? I think you can figure out who called that in."

"Jesus!" Wiegand sat silently for a moment. "I don't know who it is, man, I swear! I've only gotten notes."

"The notes must have contained enough information for you to know what it was about, right? Otherwise you wouldn't have been so quick to obey."

"I know what it's about, but I don't know who it is."

"If you tell me everything, we may be able to figure it out from there."

"I'm not talkin' 'bout that. No way!"

"Do you still have any of the notes you received?"

"Nah. They said I needed to burn 'em or they'd know. I wasn't takin' no chances."

"Okay, I guess we'll leave it at that for now, Brent. Thank you for your time. I'd like to suggest that you go to the police station and turn yourself in for the vandalism at the synagogue. All of this stuff is going to be part of my report, and it might do you some good to do it yourself, rather than getting picked up for it."

* * *

Mihdí still had an hour before he was due to meet Scott Craig. Craig lived in the north part of Pine Bluff, and Wiegand's apartment was in the south, so Mihdí headed north. He stopped in at his office, which was right on the way, and entered his latest notes into the computer. He hadn't done that for a while, so it kept him busy right up until he needed to leave to see Scott Craig.

Craig was drying his hands from doing the dishes from his late breakfast when he answered the door. He ushered Mihdí into his living room, and they sat opposite each other.

"Mr. Craig, I've got a few questions that have come up, based on conversations I've had with a few other people. I appreciate you taking the time to meet with me."

"I'm always happy to help, Detective. What do you need to know?"

"When we first spoke, I believe you told me that you and Tammy Ornstein had 'gone out for a while.' Was your relationship perhaps a bit deeper than that?"

"I guess we were pretty serious for a while."

"Pretty serious?"

"Yeah."

"Tammy told me that you two were engaged. Is that what you call 'pretty serious'?"

"Yes, we were engaged. I don't like to talk about it because Tammy broke it off. Makes me look like a loser, doesn't it?"

"What was your relationship like after Tammy broke off your engagement? Did you still talk to each other? You saw each other at Temple from time to time, right?"

"We didn't talk much. When I saw her at the synagogue, I'd say 'hello,' but not much else."

"Did you call her sometimes?"

"A few times at first, I guess. I haven't called her lately."

"Did she ever call you?"

"Not that I can remember."

"OK, I've heard enough lies. Tammy told me that she called you on the day that Jacob Klemme was killed. Given that you went to her office shortly after that, I'd have to say she's more believable than you are."

Mihdí waited. Craig was staring at him, shocked.

"This game is over, Scott," Mihdí continued. "I want the truth from now on, or I will arrest you for obstruction. Let's hear the whole story this time, with no variations from the truth."

Craig was ready to make an angry response, but Mihdí looked at him squarely in the eye without blinking. Craig seemed to think better of it. He looked down and sat quietly for a few moments, while Mihdí waited.

"OK," Craig said at last. "Yes, Tammy called me that morning. She said that she and Klemme were going to get engaged, and she wanted me to know about it ahead of time so I wouldn't go ballistic or something. It was a short conversation, because I was too angry to say much. After I hung up, I just sat there stewing about it. I decided I'd go over and try to talk to her about it."

"For what purpose?"

"To talk her out of it! We've known each other since we were kids. We belong together. Everybody knows that, including Tammy. When she broke up with me, I thought it was just some short-term thing and that she'd get over it. Then, when she was dating the rabbi, I thought that was just some rebound thing and that she'd eventually tire of him and come back to me. But when she called me to say they were getting engaged, it seemed like she was playing that game a little too seriously. I just wanted to tell her that I still loved her and wanted to be with her."

"What time was all of this?"

"Um, she must have called at maybe 10:30am. I just was paralyzed for a long time, then I left and drove over there. I must have arrived a bit before noon or something like that. It was midday, so the traffic was heavy."

"And then?"

"Well, I talked to her, like I said. I told her I wanted her to be happy and that I was the one who could do that best. I was thinking of all the good times we had. I just wanted to get her to feel good and remember what a great couple we make. I thought it was going well. I thought maybe she'd change her mind or at least postpone the engagement or something. I thought she was happy I was calling her bluff and that I'd get her back."

"But . . ."

"But then she told me that she wasn't going to change her mind and that she was still planning to marry Klemme."

"How did that make you feel?"

"How do you think? It pissed me off. I don't even know what I said after that. I must have told her she was making a mistake, and probably a lot worse than that. I was yelling and pacing back and forth, and I don't know what I said. She just sat there and looked at me—a little scared, maybe. At some point, I noticed that other people around were reacting, and I left. I sat in my car for a while, trying to calm down, but it wasn't working very well."

"You haven't said when you made an appointment to see Rabbi Klemme. How did that happen?"

"Oh, I forgot that part. I called him from my office, before I left to see Tammy. I was still hopeful at that time, but I thought if things didn't go well with Tammy, I might still have a chance to sway him a little."

"Alright. That sounds reasonable. So, you were sitting in your car, trying to calm down, but you were still quite agitated. What did you do?"

Craig stared at the floor and said quietly, "I used my phone to find the nearest gun shop and went to buy a gun."

Mihdí raised his eyebrows at that, but he didn't say anything.

Craig continued, "I'm sure you know that there's a three-day waiting period."

Mihdí nodded.

"Well, I didn't know that until I got there. I was thinking I could threaten Klemme and get him to break it off with Tam. But then I realized I couldn't buy a gun that same day, so I just left."

"Where did you go?"

"I knew I wasn't going to be able to get any work done, so I went home. The more I thought about not being able to get a gun, the angrier I got. I decided I'd look on the Internet to see if there was some way I could get around the waiting period. I must have spent three hours looking, but didn't find anything."

"Was it time for you to go meet Rabbi Klemme by then?"

"Not quite. I got myself a snack and listened to NPR for a while. Then I drove over to the synagogue and found Klemme's body, like I told you before."

"Did you do your gun searching on that computer on the desk over there?"

"Yeah, why?"

"May I take a quick look at it?"

"I suppose, why?"

"I just want to take a quick look at the browsing history, to see if there's any evidence to support your story."

"Oh, I see. OK."

Mihdí checked the browser's history and saw a number of sites that could have supplied information about getting guns. The times shown for the various site visits were consistent with Craig's story.

As he prepared to leave, Mihdí spoke directly to Craig, "Lying to the police and obstructing a murder investigation are serious crimes. I don't know yet where this case will end up, but I know that you've made it harder for me and consequently harder for yourself."

Mihdí paused. When he spoke again, his voice was quiet. "I think you are lying to yourself as well, Mr. Craig."

Craig looked up at him, with surprise showing in his eyes and something else. Fear.

"Ask yourself this question," Mihdí continued, his voice still quiet, his eyes focused on Craig's. "Had you been able to buy that gun and visit Rabbi Klemme, what would you have done if things had not gone as you thought they would? What decision would you have made if Rabbi Klemme had told you that he would keep seeing Tammy, despite you pointing your gun at him? Would you have simply put the gun away, thanked him, and walked away?"

Craig was looking down. He didn't meet Mihdí's gaze.

Mihdí let the silence draw out, then said, "You should consider yourself very lucky that there's a waiting period for buying guns, because you'd be facing a life in prison if you had gone there, threatened him, and then let your jealousy get the better of you. Get yourself some help, because next time, your luck may have run out."

When he had spoken to Tammy, Mihdí had been struck by the timing of the planned announcement of Jacob and Tammy's engagement, and he had started revising his thinking about why the murder had happened when it did. But he didn't have sufficient evidence to arrest Craig immediately. He took down the name of the gun retailer that Craig had visited and drove back to the office. He asked Kurt Childs to check whether the staff at Freddie Bear could verify that part of Craig's story.

After about fifteen minutes, Kurt came to Mihdí's office.

"The manager at Freddie Bear remembers Mr. Craig very well. He said that if there hadn't been a three-day waiting period, they would have created one for Craig. He wanted a gun, and he let them know it. He yelled at the guy helping him and demanded to see the manager. When the manager confirmed that there was a waiting period, Craig cussed him up and down. They finally threatened to call the police before they could get him to leave."

"None of that sounds the least bit surprising. Thanks, Kurt."

"Oh, by the way, this finally just came in for you from New Lenox. It's the file about that murder where they interviewed Brent Wiegand."

"Great, thanks. I hope it has something useful in it. I feel like I'm chasing whirlwinds on this case."

* * *

The file contained a number of documents, which Mihdí glanced through. He decided to start his reading with the autopsy report on the victim, Silas Pattison. The cause of death was identified as a stab wound that entered the victim just under the ribs and went upwards. No murder weapon was found. In addition to the stab wounds, there was some evidence of abuse on the body, such as might have been caused by some physical abuse, perhaps hard slaps, punches, and a few kicks. These all appeared to have been inflicted near the time of death.

The murder took place at the end of Sycamore Lane, a cul-de-sac not far from the New Lenox downtown. Gary Stevenson, the witness who had placed Wiegand in the area, had been out walking his dachshund a bit after dusk and had seen Wiegand walking ahead of him, heading east along Wood Street. He noticed that Wiegand appeared to be a bit intoxicated, but not incapacitated. At one point Wiegand picked up a pine cone from the sidewalk and was tossing it up in the air as he walked. Inevitably, he eventually dropped it, and Stevenson got a very good look at him when he turned around to pick it up. Stevenson was still behind him when Wiegand turned north on Gum Street, and he saw him enter Sycamore Lane. Stevenson lived at the outlet of Sycamore and knew it was a dead end, so he thought it was quite unusual to have someone he didn't know walk that way. He kept half an eye on the street from his kitchen window for the next fifteen minutes or so, but he did not see Wiegand come back out, so he assumed he was visiting someone. He was able to give a very good description of Wiegand's clothes, hair, face, and tattoos.

Based on Gary Stevenson's information, the New Lenox detective had correctly surmised that Wiegand had been at the VFW post, and the bartender confirmed that he had been there. The bartender also knew Brent's friend, who was a member. When they followed up with the friend, he was able to direct them to Wiegand.

The detective had interviewed Brent within twenty-four hours of the murder. Wiegand said he was trying to get to the Rock Island train station so he could go home but that he took a wrong turn. He admitted he was on Sycamore Lane but said when he got to the end of the street, he just continued through the woods and ended up back on Wood Street, the same route he had already taken. This time he got the directions right, found the train station, and went straight home. There was surveillance video at the train station that showed Wiegand on the platform about forty-five minutes after sunset. The train station is a bit more than a twenty-minute walk from the murder site, so it was still possible for Wiegand to have committed the murder, but getting through the woods in his impaired condition might well have slowed him down enough to account for the additional time. There was no other evidence that tied Wiegand to the crime, so they had not pursued him further.

Mihdí flipped through the other pages in the file to see if there was any other information of interest. On one page, the name "Richardson" caught his eye. It was the initial report of the crime, which had been called in by Charles Richardson, a real estate agent from Pine Bluff. Richardson had come in to work on a house on Sycamore Lane the morning after the murder had apparently been committed. He had seen the body lying just off the street, in the grassy area in the center of the turnaround at the end of the lane, and had called the police immediately.

When he was interviewed later, Richardson told the detectives that he had been working at the house the evening before but had to leave shortly after dusk because the power was turned off, so he didn't have sufficient light to keep working. He couldn't say whether the body was there when he left, as he had pulled straight out of the driveway and up the lane, not around the circle, and had been on the wrong side of his truck to notice a body in the gloom. The occupants of the only house that fronted onto the turnaround, beyond the one Richardson was working on, were gone on vacation.

The interview form included Richardson's address, which was on the 14600 block of Darwin Avenue. Mihdí checked the address on his computer, as he didn't recognize the street. It was, as Richardson had told him, less than half a mile west of his office. A thought occurred to him, so Mihdí checked his notes from his interview with Meredith and Barry Grant, the couple Richardson had escorted around Pine Bluff to look at houses on the Tuesday of last week. They had provided Richardson with an alibi during the estimated hours of Rabbi Klemme's murder. According to them, Richardson had told them that his children attended Bluff Point Elementary School. But because Richardson lived west of Pine Bluff's main street, Mihdí realized that couldn't be the case; they would have started at Pulaski Elementary and then moved to Emmett Till Elementary when they were a bit older. Mihdí was also conscious that when he had talked to Richardson this morning, the real estate agent had seemed to be in a big hurry to get away from him to meet the Grants, and wondered if that had been on purpose.

Mihdí immediately called Richardson's cell phone, but it went straight to voice mail. He looked up Meredith Grant's cell phone number, and she picked up right away.

"Mrs. Grant?"

"Yes. Who is this?"

"Please don't call me by name just now, but this is Detective Mihdí Montgomery."

"OK," she said with a puzzled voice. "What can I do for you?"

"Please don't react in any way; just say 'yes' or 'no'—Is Charlie Richardson with you right now?"

"Yes."

"Could you tell me the address where you are?"

"Sure, it's 14116 Newark Avenue, just off Lexington Drive."

"Please just try to stay there, if at all possible. I'll be there in ten minutes."

Mihdí practically ran to the parking lot, hopped in his car, and drove. He arrived at the house in less than ten minutes. Meredith Grant was standing in the driveway by herself.

"Barry and Mr. Richardson are in the back yard, detective. I didn't say a thing to either of them. What's going on?"

"I'm not sure I know, but I need to talk to Charlie Richardson."

He went around the side of the house to where the two men were talking. Although their backs were to him, they turned around as they heard him approaching. Barry Grant was on the right, but the man on the left, although he looked very much like Charlie Richardson, was clearly someone else.

"Hello, Detective," Barry Grant said. "I'm surprised to see you here. What's up?"

"Hello, Mr. Grant. I'm actually here to speak to Mr. Richardson. Would you mind excusing us for a few minutes?"

"No problem. I need to talk to Meredith, anyway." Grant headed to the front of the house, taking the same route that Mihdí had just used.

"As you may have heard, I am Detective Mihdí Montgomery of the Pine Bluff Police Department. And you are . . . ?"

The man hesitated for a moment. "I'm John Richardson, detective, Charlie's twin brother."

"Please explain what's going on here."

John Richardson was obviously uncomfortable with being caught in a lie. His face was flushed, and he shuffled from foot to foot as he talked. "Charlie had some kind of conflict, so he asked me if I would come and show these people around the city last week. Charlie and I used to work together, and I'm a licensed real estate agent myself, so I help Charlie out now and then when he really needs it."

"But you told the Grants that you were Charlie . . ."

"Yeah, Charlie asked me if I would do that. It was a bit odd, but I assume Charlie had his reasons. He hasn't asked that in the past. It seems like a pretty harmless deception. Then, since I showed them around last week, calling myself Charlie, I pretty much had to do it again this time."

"So, when you've done this before in the past, you usually just introduced yourself as John and said you were working with Charlie, but this time he wanted you to pretend to be him."

"Yeah, I guess so."

"Did anybody else know about this arrangement?"

"Well, Ximena Gomez—that's his assistant—she certainly knows that I help Charlie out from time to time. In fact, usually she's the one who calls me to ask me to meet clients. But this time, Charlie called me himself. It's not the first time he's called me directly, but it's usually Ximena. I suppose it was because of the special request that I use his name."

"Yes, I imagine so. Do you happen to know what your brother's conflict was last week?"

"Nope, no idea. I work on my own time nowadays, so I'm happy to do something a little different. I didn't ask him why, I just said I'd be happy to do it."

"Do you know where your brother is now?"

"Nope. He might be showing a house to somebody else, but I really don't know. Is Charlie in trouble?"

Mihdí ignored the question. He handed Richardson his card. "Thank you very much for your information, Mr. Richardson. If your brother calls you, please let me know. Otherwise, I'd appreciate it if you didn't call him for a few hours."

The Grants were standing beside what he assumed must be Richardson's car as Mihdí returned to his Mini, so he gave them a wave, but he didn't stop to talk. He drove back to the police station and sat in the parking lot thinking what to do next. He called Richardson's cell phone, but again it went straight to voice mail. He called the office number and reached Ximena. He identified himself and asked her if she knew Richardson's whereabouts.

"Well, not exactly, sir," she said, "but I know he's out with a young couple from Des Plaines, taking a second look at some houses. The . . . uh . . . Grants."

"Mmm. So you haven't seen him since he left the office this morning?"

"No. I would guess he'd be done soon, though, and I'll be happy to have him call you when he gets in."

"Thanks, Ms. Gomez."

Mihdí thought about it for a few more minutes and decided he would check out the synagogue. If Richardson were involved in the murder, it would be because he wanted the congregation to sell and move out, so he might be trying to find new ways to encourage them to do that.

Mihdí went to the front door of the synagogue. Since the rabbi's death, he assumed that the front door was generally kept locked, but he tried it anyway and found it unlocked. He hoped to enter very quietly, but there was some construction noise coming from down the street, and he was afraid it could be heard inside. He opened the door a crack, very slowly. He thought he heard some small sounds from inside, but the outside noise made it impossible to tell for sure. He proceeded to push the door open a bit wider and slipped in. The front door led into the sanctuary, but there was a short wall dividing the door from the main room, so someone entering would not be seen. He quietly closed the door behind him. The sanctuary was rather dark, lit only by daylight coming through windows and through the office area door. Mihdí waited for about a minute as his eyes adjusted to the darkness.

He listened intently but did not hear anything in the sanctuary. He peered around the corner of the dividing wall and didn't detect any movement. He moved very slowly to avoid making any noise, still worried that he had heard something earlier. He crept slowly out of the entrance way toward the back rows of pews, drawing his service pistol as he walked. He remembered the light switches as being on the right side of the sanctuary, near the hallway leading to the office door, about halfway up, so he headed cautiously in that direction.

He reached the back corner of the pews and started moving up the side aisle, still moving quietly but a bit faster. He still had four or five more rows of pews to go before he reached the door leading to the office area. He stopped suddenly and looked at the wall beside him. Even in the gloom, he could see that part of a swastika had been roughly carved into the plaster wall. He looked at it a bit more closely to see if he could see what kind of tool might have been used. He also stooped to look at the floor, thinking he saw some fresh plaster dust just under the carving on the wall.

He knelt on the carpet and set his pistol on the floor so that he could examine the plaster dust more closely. Just at that moment, a figure jumped out at him from between two pews. The attacker was wielding a large hunting knife and caught Mihdí with a slash across his left shoulder. Mihdí jumped backward, away from his attacker but also a long way from his pistol, which was fortunately hidden by the darkness in the sanctuary. He was off balance, however, so he fell onto his back when he landed. The man with the knife rushed in his direction, apparently intending to land on him and complete his attack. Mihdí managed to block the attacker with his feet and pushed him back into the pews. That gave Mihdí time to get up and put some distance between himself and his assailant, as well as to draw them both away from his gun, which he hoped had escaped notice. With that distance, he could see the other man clearly in the light from the office door.

"Richardson, you're only going to make things worse for yourself."

"Don't kid yourself, detective. You're not going to be able to tell your story to anyone, and I'm going to walk out of here. Though before I do, I might carve a swastika into you, just like I did on that wall. That should put the Jews into a selling mood, eh?"

Richardson was slowly inching nearer, the knife held threateningly in front of him.

"These things never work out the way you think they will, Charlie. Put the knife down, and let's talk about it."

Charlie scoffed and took a swing at Mihdí with the knife. Mihdí was able to duck away, but he was being forced slowly into the back corner of the sanctuary. He made as if to lunge forward, but then pulled back. Richardson took the bait and made another swing at Mihdí. The detective was ready this time and leapt forward before Richardson could bring the knife back to position. He dodged Mihdí's blow, though, and skipped backwards out of Mihdí's range.

Mihdí had succeeded, though, in getting himself out of the corner, so the two of them faced each other on more equal terms. Mihdí was bleeding steadily from the wound on his shoulder, but he tried to ignore it and focus on the man in front of him.

"You blackmailed Brent Wiegand to vandalize this place and the Islamic Center, didn't you?"

"That imbecile. He was a pretty easy tool to manipulate."

As he said this, Richardson started waving the knife wildly in front of him and danced towards Mihdí. The detective grabbed a two-handled brass flower vase from a table at the back of the sanctuary and held it up as a shield as he backed away from the slashing knife. Richardson wasn't able to get close enough to Mihdí to use the knife and didn't want to take the chance of it being knocked out of his hands by the vase Mihdí was holding. Richardson quit waving the knife and again stood with it pointed at Mihdí.

"This is his knife, actually," Richardson said. "I pulled it out of the body of that homeless guy over in New Lenox. I thought that the knife, along with the video I made of Wiegand killing him, could both come in handy."

"How did you arrange that?"

"Bit of luck, actually. I was working at the house and was just getting ready to quit when I saw the two of them arguing. There was no power in the house, so I was in the dark and pretty much invisible, but they were standing right under a streetlight. I whipped out my phone and started filming."

Mihdí kicked out and just managed to connect with Richardson's wrist, but Richardson was able to hold onto the knife.

"That hurt, you worthless piece of crap! I'll make you pay for that." He lunged at Mihdí but wasn't able to make contact.

"So, you just watched Wiegand kill an innocent man and did nothing, is that it?"

"He didn't look innocent to me, just weak. Wiegand's no Schwarzenegger, but that black guy didn't even put up a fight. Wiegand looked like he just wanted to harass the guy for fun. He slapped him a few times and punched him and the guy just stood there and took it. Finally, he must have gotten fed up and he swung once or twice at Wiegand and must have hit him. Wiegand yanked this knife out of his belt or somewhere and jabbed it right between the black guy's ribs. And I got the whole thing on tape."

They continued to dance around each other, occasionally feinting or dodging, but neither one made any kind of effective attack. All of a sudden, Mihdí threw the vase at Richardson's head and followed up with a rush towards the real estate agent. Richardson ducked away from the vase, but was unable to avoid Mihdí's charge. The two of them went down, locked in each other's arms, with Mihdí on top. Mihdí was holding Richardson's right wrist with his left hand, but he could feel his left shoulder weakening from the deep cut. He rolled to his left, pinning Richardson's right shoulder and arm beneath him so he could not use the knife. Mihdí swung his left elbow into Richardson's right side, then raised his arm and brought it down on Richardson's throat. Mihdí was unable to provide any continued pressure, though, because of his weakened shoulder.

Richardson, with his right armed trapped under Mihdí's body, was flailing around ineffectually, landing a few feeble blows with his left hand, but unable to get any leverage. He tried to pull his right arm out from under Mihdí. He grabbed the leg of a heavy table with his left hand to anchor himself and tried to dislodge the detective. Mihdí saw that both of Richardson's arms were out of the way, so he swung his right arm around and rolled a bit so he could deliver a chop on Richardson's throat with his right hand. He was at a difficult angle, so the chop wasn't particularly hard or well-placed, but it did cause Richardson some pain and he gasped for breath. Mihdí was able to roll forward and get to his feet, avoiding a wild swing of the knife. Richardson propped himself up on his left elbow, still brandishing the knife, but he was still too winded to be able to get up quickly. Mihdí hauled himself to the front door and exited the synagogue. He didn't stop when he got outside, but stumbled over to Ahmad Muhammad's coffee shop, where he collapsed in the doorway. Ahmad didn't immediately know the identity of the injured man limping past his window, but he sprinted for the door as soon as he saw him and got there just moments after Mihdí had fallen. He yanked open the door and knelt down next to him.

At that moment, Richardson emerged from the synagogue and saw the tableau in the coffee shop doorway. He began to run toward the two men with the knife held out in front of him, still struggling a bit for breath. Mihdí saw him first and yelled a warning to Muhammad, pointing to Richardson.

The coffee shop owner leapt fearlessly to his feet facing Charlie Richardson and stood so that he was completely shielding Mihdí. Richardson stopped in his tracks, as it began to dawn on him that his plan was crumbling.

The noise of Mihdí's shout had brought other curious people to the doors of their shops. Stephanie Plante emerged from the HisStory bookstore and hurried over to Uncommon Brews. While Ahmad Muhammad continued to stare Richardson down, she attended to Mihdí. With her help, the detective was able to stand up and face his erstwhile attacker.

"Put your weapon down, Richardson," he commanded, leaning heavily against the doorframe of the coffee shop. "It's over. Stephanie, could you please call 911?"

Richardson looked around slowly, then tossed the knife down on the sidewalk and took a few steps away from it.

"I had no choice, Montgomery," he said dejectedly. "I'm so far in debt I needed this project to get back on my feet."

Mihdí could feel anger beginning to well up inside him, but he spoke calmly. "You always have a choice, Richardson. Sometimes the choices are hard, but there are always choices. And you made bad ones. You made Jacob Klemme and Silas Pattison pay for your bad choices, and now you'll make your family pay as well, for years to come. And you yourself will always pay, as long as you don't take responsibility for every choice you make."

Ahmad was unwilling to leave Mihdí unprotected, but a customer brought a chair out for Mihdí, who slumped gratefully into it. It took only three minutes for the police to arrive, followed quickly by an ambulance. Kurt Childs arrived just a few minutes after the first officers. He consulted quickly with Mihdí to get the latest facts, then formally arrested Richardson and led him to a patrol car. He dispatched the patrol car with Richardson in it to the police department lockup and bundled Mihdí off in the ambulance to the hospital.

Childs oversaw the quick clean-up of the case. Richardson told them where to find the DVD of the video of Brent Wiegand stabbing Silas Pattison. Contrary to Mihdí's earlier suggestion, Wiegand had not turned himself in. Officers were sent to his home, where he was arrested and charged with murder and obstruction, on top of the charges for vandalism of the Islamic Center and the Beth Shalom synagogue. Richardson's list of charges was even longer.

* * *

Mihdí needed fourteen stitches in his shoulder, but was treated and released before suppertime. Sam Schliebaum had called Andrea that afternoon to make a special request for the whole family to come to the Interfaith Community Thanksgiving Service at the synagogue that evening. Although Mihdí was still in a lot of pain and Andrea was concerned about him overexerting himself, he was happy for a good reason to go. They arrived almost exactly at 7:30. Schliebaum met them at the door and ushered them to a front row seat. The service began immediately, before Mihdí even got a chance to look around.

Representatives of various local religious groups took turns with the various parts of the service. An interfaith choir sang two numbers, conducted by the Music Director of Saint Luke United Methodist Church. Prayers were offered, songs were sung, and scriptures were read. When the time came for the homily, Sam Schliebaum came to the front to share some thoughts on the occasion of Thanksgiving. He stood silently for a moment before he began.

"I'm sure you have all noticed the unfinished swastika on the wall. This act of desecration of our sanctuary came on the heels of the murder in this very room of our friend and colleague, Jacob Klemme, just last week. These four walls almost witnessed another murder here this afternoon. We left the swastika here to witness the gathering of people of goodwill from all around our city in this service this evening. Soon after the service is over, we will take steps to remove this symbol of hate, as our innocent belief in the safety and purity of our sanctuary has already been forcibly removed.

"But we have also gained something that is perhaps of more significance. We have gained a new appreciation for the importance of what we're doing here tonight. Through this interfaith service, we are building bonds of friendship and respect between members of different religions. Like many of you, I have long believed that building bridges between people of faith is important. We have had services every year, and we have, from time to time, welcomed each other into our rituals and worship. These things have been good, and they have served to make us all feel like members of a larger congregation than our own, a congregation of all of God's people in every land on earth.

"Today, though, through the work of my friend, Detective Mihdí Montgomery, I have a new idea of what it means to build bonds between people of faith. It can't be done just in annual services and occasional visits to other people's houses of worship. It must be done in the day-to-day acceptance and honoring of every person created by the Almighty. It must be done by learning about each other's religions, each other's cultures, and each other's values. And it must also be done by learning about each other's families and children and interests and each other's hopes and fears. My friend has taught me this not by preaching but by doing. His work today may have saved our synagogue and perhaps some of our lives. But I believe his work every day has helped to strengthen our community. And it has given new meaning to interfaith work for me, and I hope it will for you as well."

He came over to where Mihdí was sitting. "Detective, would you join me here for a moment?"

Schliebaum helped Mihdí stand and turn to face the congregation, which burst into applause. With tears in his eyes, Mihdí saw that just behind Andrea, Enoch, and Lua, Ahmad Muhammad was sitting with a young woman, probably his wife. Stephanie Plante was sitting on the other side of the aisle with Sandy Klarr and a visibly uncomfortable Matthew Skefton. As Mihdí looked out at the still applauding crowd, he spotted Harry Katz and Neil Hoffman. Ruth Fischbach was sitting near Scott Craig. Mihdí saw his friends Ray Engel, Janice Chernievski, and Erica Iyer. His neighbor, Karen Short, was on the left, while Jill Bartholomew was on the right. A few police colleagues were there, including Darla Brownlee and Kurt Childs. Rick Sapp sat between his sons, Carl and Andy, neither of whom looked particularly happy about being there. Mihdí also picked out Brenda Lyons and the Rouhanis from his local Bahá'í community, as well as many other friends.

As the applause began to die down, Schliebaum asked, "Would you say a few words, Mihdí?"

Mihdí nodded and cast his eyes around the room. "A Muslim, a Christian, a Jew, and a Bahá'í walked into a coffee shop," he began. When the inevitable laughter died down, he continued, "That shouldn't be as unusual as it seems that it is. We all like coffee. We all have families. We all share many values. We all try to live our lives in the ways we think best. And when we do those things together, we all feel stronger connections to our communities, to our families, to our faith, and to our God. Those connections are a protection, a comfort and an amazing gift. And that is something that's definitely worth giving thanks for."

Mihdí stood for a moment, his eyes filling with tears. His daughter, Lua, seeing her father crying, jumped from her seat and rushed over to him. He bent over to catch her in his right arm and lifted her up, where she gave him a big hug. Andrea hadn't been fast enough to stop Lua, but she followed, with Enoch close behind. Enoch hugged his father's legs while Andrea took Lua from Mihdí, who was beginning to show that he was feeling his fatigue and the pain of his injury.

Andrea turned to Sam Schliebaum and said, "I hope you will excuse us, but I think our hero needs to get some rest."

She took Mihdí's hand and began to lead him towards the rear of the synagogue. The congregation stood, row by row, as Mihdí walked past, silently expressing their admiration and love.

Andrea drove the family home and got the children ready for bed while Mihdí rested on the couch. Both kids came and sat next to their Dad while he read them a bedtime story. The children got their goodnight hugs and kisses from Mihdí, then their mother took them off to bed.

By the time she came downstairs, Mihdí was nodding off where he sat on the couch. She sat down next to him, put a pillow on her lap, and guided his head to it, where he quickly fell asleep. Andrea sat quietly, gently caressing his hair as he slept. At about 10 p.m., she woke him to say it was time they went up to bed.

"Why now?" he quipped, with a smile.

She laughed, "That's the big question, isn't it?"

He leaned on her shoulder as they made their way up the stairs to the bedroom.